Thomas Keneally

Thomas Keneally was born in 1935 and was educated in Sydney. He trained for several years for the Catholic priesthood but did not take orders. In a distinguished writing career he has had four novels shortlisted for the Booker Prize, which he won in 1982 with SCHINDLER'S ARK – since made by Steven Spielberg into the internationally acclaimed film, *Schindler's List*. He has also written several works of non-fiction, including most recently A YEAR IN THE ANTIPODES, about growing up in Sydney. His latest novel, A RIVER TOWN, is also published by Sceptre.

SCEPTRE

Also by Thomas Keneally and published by Sceptre

By The Line

THOMAS KENEALLY

SCEPTRE

First published in 1965 in Australia by Cassell as *The Fear*
Revised edition published in 1989 by University of Queensland Press
Published in 1992 in Great Britain by Hodder and Stoughton Ltd
A Sceptre Paperback

10 9 8 7 6 5 4

British Library Cataloguing in Publication Data

A CIP catalogue record for this book is
available from the British Library

ISBN 0 340 56231 5

Printed and bound in Great Britain by
Cox and Wyman Ltd, Reading, Berkshire

Hodder and Stoughton
A division of Hodder Headline PLC
338 Euston Road
London NW1 3BH

To my mother
who was not Stell,
but better.

1

Next door to us lay the Mantles' narrow little brick place. Both to east and west it was crowded by larger structures, ours and someone else's. Like an ill-laid tombstone, it seemed to be subsiding crookedly into the earth, and was a sunless warren, dim humidity in summer, dim moisture in winter. The laneway to its back door ran flush against our side wall and, blocked off from the light, the moss on the Mantles' lounge room window sill grew a quarter of an inch thick.

Len Mantle and Hilda must have been in their early thirties and had two boys to boast of — though *boast* is in this case a cruel word. For the younger one was, physically at least, a slack-mouthed replica of his slack-mouthed father, and *that* was nothing to boast of; while the elder had some congenital disease of the nervous system which was, cell by cell, turning his muscles to jelly and making him walk on the balls of his feet, in what many people who did not know believed to be an insane parody of elegance.

Our old home, my parents' and mine, had been no more than four hundred miles northwards and not even in another state. Still our migration plunged me into shock. The heat was duller. The air was full of sweat. By night I choked with asthma. By day I haunted the yard, not believing that from it you couldn't sight a brown elbow of river, Guernseys cropping an emerald flood-plain, the smoke-blue tangle of New England hills. My eyes constantly returned to a galvanised iron fence, and beyond it the brick butt-ends of shop residences. In-evitably, Hilda saw me, and judging me merely lonely, told my mother to send me in to meet the boys.

It wasn't long before I explored that fungoid lane which led towards the squabbling noise of the Mantles at play with each other in their overgrown backyard. (As Len Mantle was to say, a man with a cause has no time to muck about with lawnmowers.) They sat on flattened grass beneath an old peach tree, arguing over a bow made out of a peach sapling by their almighty father. Their small angry heads nodded polemically. Their hair was straight, fine, Asiatic hair, as if their grandmother had known a Chinaman; and as they spoke, it flopped over their foreheads in wads. There was an Asiatic smoothness and roundness about their faces too, and the corners of their eyes were taut. No direct acknowledgment of my existence in their own backyard was made, but all the heat went out of their squabble. They began to perform their argument, and I, knowing my place, stood by, showing polite interest as it developed.

"You let the bloody string go loose," the younger one hissed, pausing for me to marvel at the adjective. "Comrade Lenin told you not to, he told you how to keep it tight, he told you you could use it even! But off he goes to work and you spoil it on me! Now we have to wait for Comrade Lenin to make us another one, and he might be too busy to make it for years. Comrade, I could kick your guts in!"

The elder brother, Joe, was sitting with his long legs and abnormally arched feet tucked under him. For a while he kept silence for he understood that Lennie, the other one, was just a young buck rattling his spears. What he did not understand, what I did not know, was that he was, in strict truth, sitting on death, that the enemy of his blood and his genes was, at that moment, under the peach tree, seducing his nerves, lulling his muscles to reflexless blubber. He leant across towards Lennie, picked up the bow and flexed it, knobbly elbows splayed out from his sides, for the enemy was in his arms as well.

"Who said *you* owned it?" he asked. "I remember the day he made this. He made it for me. I didn't ever say you could use it."

Lennie leant forward and roared in his brother's face, "You stinking big liar, Joseph. *I* helped the Comrade make this bloody bow on a day you had the pains. He made it for *me*. Why would he make it for a bloke who can't even walk proper?"

Joseph squinted savagely at the insult, rolled it over on his tongue, spat it out onto the grass. Lennie was wise enough to sit back, waiting for the argument to sprout a new limb.

"The time he made another bow and arrow," Joseph said at length, "he let me cut it off the tree with his own knife." This was answer complete, this was fulfilment, to cut a bough with the Comrade's own knife.

"I was too small to cut it then. That's the only reason. He felt my muscles and said I was a real son to have. He told me he always wants *me* to cut his wood, right until I die."

Joseph had the calm certitude of mountains and icebergs. His anger was a queer wise anger that gave what he said neither heat nor eloquence but the sting of truth.

"He wouldn't say that. You're six. Who'd talk to a six-year-old as if he was important. I can tell you, Lennie, I'm as good as a grown-up to the Comrade. You're a baby of a six-year-old. Grown-ups tell babies anything. They even tell them Santa Claus."

Perhaps Lennie *did* lose his self-control there. He yelled and ground his teeth and hurled himself on his brother. Nature had provided for an even fight — Lennie's short strong limbs tangling with Joseph's weak long ones. The two rolled on the crushed yellow grass in what was more like brotherly love than anger.

As they grunted at my feet, and Lennie spat maniac hate through clenched teeth, I saw that I had the balance of power and decided to use it in a statesmanlike manner. To throw myself in on Joseph's side, down I dropped on that bundle of melodramatically writhing limbs, that vortex of hisses and threats. Joseph's right arm had been flung wide of the fight and lay along the grass abnormally long, like a pallid eel. I knelt on it. Joseph screamed, and Lennie, about to deal some death blow or other, became immediately still and stared at me.

"Don't touch my brother," he growled — not forcefully enough to warrant hostilities though, since I was taller than he was. He rose from where he had been sitting on Joseph's diaphragm. "Don't be so cruel."

I progressed on my knees off Joseph's arm, embarrassed at the fierce little face glaring at me over Joseph flat on the ground, groaning detachedly.

"The Comrade will belt the tripes out of you for being cruel to Joseph."

The victim raised himself on his elbows and nodded. Comrade Lenin, about whose exact nature I was still guessing, was something worth placating, said the nod.

4

"My brother Joseph," Lennie went on with pride, "is going to be a cripple. His muscles will squeeze up. And then he's going to die."

I stared at Joseph's legs, looking for some horrific sign on their lengthy whiteness.

"It won't hurt," Joseph explained. His face was gratified; his little brother had recognised him as a child of election.

"Are you really going to die?" I asked him.

"Too right!" he said. "What's your name?"

After a while there was another brawl and I was allowed to join in, fighting at will on both sides.

Sunlight had left the yard and the flaccid grass was cold. Wrestling had overheated me, given me croup, making my under-jaw itch in that unscratchable penetrating way that croup does. We were all standing around talking limply when Hilda appeared in the back door, her hair newly combed and her face done up. Her fragrance carried as far as the peach tree.

"Comrade Lenin's train just passed," she called. It was rarely that she could predict the Comrade's coming, rarely and by a hard road; for only after a furniture-breaking brawl, a bout of repentance, a promise of eternal domesticity by the Comrade, could his wife be sure, for a day or two, of when she would see him and in what state.

Of course, that afternoon I didn't know all this. Lennie and Joseph appeared to me to be people established in their neighbourhood. Out of the peach tree and the rank backyard, out of the *to and fro* of trains, the *to and fro* of Comrade Lenin, they seemed to have compounded for themselves a ritual day. They herded the hours along under firm control. They waved at the trains as if every man and woman on board were their godparents. They didn't blush when the best they earned from any carriage in a long series of dusk electrics was a few half-turned, blank faces. They were happy. Comrade Lenin was on his way home to them.

In a tweedy old sportscoat, grey trousers, and boots, he appeared out of the last knot of people stamping down the street away from the station. In his breast pocket he wore an enviable blood-red handkerchief embroidered with a white hammer and sickle. He was clearly a relative of theirs; I was still uncertain whether he was their father or not.

Lennie ran to him, Joseph stalked up to him on the balls of those extraordinary feet. As they approached him, he stood still and clenched his fist towards the sky, while a passing typist ducked below the indiscriminate gesture and hurried away.

"Hail Comrades!" he called to the boys.

"Hail Comrade!" they sang.

"Did you have any fights today, Comrades?" he asked, as if training them in the ways of peace were his prime work.

"No fear!" said Lennie.

"Good!" said Comrade Lenin.

As he came through the gateway, I jumped aside, half-hoping he hadn't even seen me.

"And did you behave yourself for the Mother of the People?"

"I did! Not Joseph!"

By now we were trailing the great man down his dim laneway. He reached his hand out onto Lennie's straight hair and lovingly tousled it.

"You're a character, Comrade! You're a heck of a character!"

We walked forward into sunlight. Comrade Lenin met Hilda with suspect ardour. I wondered if he came

6

home daily, for there was something forced and dishonest in their embrace, something feigned like the feigned anger that had flung the boys against each other earlier that afternoon. I can remember now that probably a dozen kitchen windows in flats and cottages looked down on the Mantles' backyard, flats and cottages where rumours of the Comrade's drinking, violence, shiftlessness were harboured. Hilda was a proud girl.

Even now, she looked up at him and murmured, "You've been having some."

"Only a nip," he grunted, and they went inside.

"Why does he wear a red handkerchief?" I asked the boys.

"That's his colour," said Lennie. "It's the colour of the Soviet flag."

"The people's flag is deepest red," Joseph explained. "Didn't you know that?"

"Yes!" I lied.

"It's bathed in the blood of the workers."

"Is his handkerchief bathed in their blood?"

"Yes," Lennie whispered.

"When did he bathe it in their blood?"

"After they'd been shot in the back by someone. The catilists." Joseph was bland in his knowledge of whence the workers' blood flowed.

"Why did they shoot them?"

"They were scared of them."

"Is Comrade Lenin a worker?"

"He's one of the leaders of the workers."

"Then why didn't they shoot him?"

"He ran away?" Lennie suggested.

Joseph sneered at this. "He didn't run away. They thought he was dead but he wasn't. There was a soldier like that at the pictures."

"Soldier like what?" Comrade Lenin had come into

the yard in his slippers. He was in his shirtsleeves, the coat and the bloody handkerchief being away somewhere deep in the Mantle house. I could imagine some sort of reliquary, with candles flanking it, for that piece of linen which had been dipped in precious blood.

"You've got a new mate," he observed. His eyes flapped across my face with gross indifference. There was something about me which made me unfit to pluck a bow, yell or spit, roll and wrestle with his comrades. I was a bit livid and narrow-chested, I admitted to myself, from pneumonia the previous November.

"What's your name, youngster?"

"Daniel Jordan."

"Well, Daniel Jordan," he said, slicing my name up with the thin edge of his tongue, "you'd better go home. I'm taking the boys for a walk. You can come back tomorrow."

"Yes."

"Well, be seeing you! Joseph? Lennie?"

They followed him into a kitchen redolent of lamb chop fat. Now I had the whole yard, but mere possession was meaningless without them. Dusk dropped from the peach tree, the lane lay before me like a catacomb. Running its length, I was standing on our veranda in time to see the Comrade usher his sons into the street and take them uphill. Lennie yabbered at his side, Joseph stalked forward as if the ground were strewn with nettles. They reached a point at last where trees and railway embankment, the coming night and steam from a reined-in engine all blended into utter shadow.

2

Then Singapore fell. The very sucklings quaked for its fall. A Cabinet Minister whispered in committee that one armoured division could take Australia. People taped their windows, making them shatterproof, prophesying that the only human factor that could save us was America. Women sought moral guidance on the question of suicide or dishonour. Troops trained with sticks and guarded beachheads with axes.

Bombs homed down on London and corpses were dug out each morning. That was true. Yet no country was ever so naked before invasion as the Australia of 1942.

Civil defence men came to school to teach us to out-hide, out-wriggle, out-delve death from the sky. We were to have white linen bags, to be worn on the hip and to contain a bisected tennis ball (for cupping to your outraged ears as you lay in the gutter during the bombing), a plug of gauze (to bite into), a bandage, and a tin of salve. In answer to the unopposed Japanese armaments, we held up our tins of salve and, since these were primarily suitable for chillblains, ant-bite and minor burns, it was as well for us that they never had to be opened.

9

Beneath the high altar of the church was the school air-raid shelter. There were two reasons for its location. The playground itself was asphalted and the nuns hesitated to set a pick to its even surface: and then, in that dark hole, we were mantled and protected by the table of God. It was unlikely, the nuns said, that the Sacred Species would be allowed to suffer bombing. In a lavender-painted classroom, with the windows half-open and a yellow surf of boronia breaking on the sills, this reasoning had obvious strength.

We were all sent to the toilets and then lined up in the corridors to practise in our shelter. The entry was a squat green manhole inlaid in the prosperous brick of the apse's outer wall. Sister Eucheria of the Order of Preachers, the ancient Dominicans, smiled plump encouragement back along the flighty column of infants, unlocked the door and stooped down into the darkness within. In her supernaturally cream habit, Sister Stanislaus waited behind in the sunlight to soothe the atavistic panic we all felt in regard to doors you had to bend to enter and beyond which lay what might be the blackness of the pit.

"Keep on coming!" Stanislaus called masterfully, and if that dark cellar had been the foyer of hell, we would have willingly faced its minor terrors rather than oppose her.

Within, the shelter was a place where odd lengths of lumber and camp tables used for Communion breakfasts were kept. There was even an electric bulb which Sister Eucheria had turned on. She ushered me to the far penumbra of its cone of bilious light, and I sat on a stack of tables with some other, mainly solemn, children. From here, the light seemed paltry, the whole place incredibly dim, low-roofed, weighed down. Weighed down by the weight of divinity above our heads, constricted by the acres of darkness on three sides of us, the little pad of daylight which was the doorway seemed furlongs away, and the inpouring bodies of another and another child blotted it out. My chest became tight, whistled with a congestion to match the congestion of this *sub-altare* into which an intolerable stream of children thronged.

"Isn't it cold?" Dolph Conlon whispered, as if we were fleas on the flanks of darkness and didn't want it to scratch itself.

"I'm not going to come in here," I wheezed, "even if the Japs bomb the school."

"Sister Stanislaus'll make you."

"I'll hide till she comes in here."

"Then where'll you hide? From all those bombs?"

"I'll hide . . ." If the bombers came languidly across the sky, Eucheria would probably send us to the toilets before consigning us to the abyss. The boys' toilets were corrugated tin and unfit to perish in, being utterly abandoned to the lower uses of what Mother Gonzaga called the *bhoys*. But this austerity outhouse was an apter place to die in than down there choking in the pit. To die in a blitz amongst the corrugated iron, flung across the durable chalk-line which God or, more binding still, Stanislaus had drawn along the floor, and behind which no *bhoy* was to stand while performing a natural function; that would be a joy beside surviving the smallest bombardment vaulted beneath the High Altar.

"Haven't you got any faith?" Dolph asked me. Before I could explain myself, Dolph stood up from our pile of tables and, with a little groan, delivered himself of his lunch.

Air-raid practice next occurred on a grey April afternoon. The glossy reading books were collected and, swept along by a tide of blithe colleagues, I drifted into the toilets and out again to find myself, swallowing on a tongue parched with fear, being marched off to the small green door.

Glossy-leaved eucalypts looked with odious calm at the line of children embarking into the labyrinth. An old lady limped out of the presbytery door and poured a basin of dishwater down a drain. In her warm bubble of domesticity she didn't even bother to glance at us. Low cloud shut mercy out of the sky, and I stared down the nave, begging mercy to turn the corner. Incredibly, it did.

Walking very fast and splendid in her best-wear brown suit, my mother arrived. I pretended not to see her, but a girl at the top of the line touched Stanislaus' cream-serge elbow and pointed towards the splendid apparition. The nun looked up and smiled.

"I've come to get Daniel, Sister," my mother said. "I thought you mightn't have heard."

"Heard, Mrs Jordan?" Without waiting to be answered Stanislaus turned towards the line and called me. As I idled up the side of the ranks, I heard my mother say in half-whisper, "There's been a Jap bomber over Sydney. High up. Our grocer's a warden and he was alerted. It's probably gone now, but I'd like to take Daniel if you don't mind."

Eucheria pushed her head out of the black hole.

"Oh, good afternoon, Mrs Jordan."

"Sister," said Stanislaus, "a Japanese aircraft has been sighted over Sydney. I wish we could send all the children home, but Father's out and we'd have to have his permission. Anyway, their parents wouldn't know what was happening."

"Oh, I don't think there's any great danger yet," my mother frowned. "But, if anything happened, you'd like to have them with you, I mean, parents would, wouldn't they?"

"Yes. By all means, take him. The best we can do, Sister Eucheria, is to go on with our air-raid practice."

My mother and I walked away and turned for a shy second to wave to the children and Stanislaus. Even to my eyes, Dolph Conlon seemed a small and pale animal, in acute need of a mother. For a moment, I shuddered with the ecstacy of deliverance, the shame of being the only one delivered. Then we began to hurry home.

For every yard of the quiet avenues which separated us from the railway and our place, we searched the shut-in sky. Two American fighters jumped over the western skyline and hummed beneath the dome of cloud — comforting, blood-stirring, silver, blue and red.

"Why didn't they shoot it down?" I asked, and despite the flamboyant Americans holding our attention, my mother didn't mistake whom I meant by *they*.

"They could have been having lunch," she said, "or having an hour off. Anyhow, it was a long way up. And it's only one Jap plane. Hardly worth bothering about."

Since I had begun school, an idea which was probably hereditary had grown to become a premise of life. It was the idea of the large world, the school-world in particular, as a conspiracy to scrape bare all the weaknesses of the soul, to mock the indomitable tenderness of the secret, family world, making them baseless, unmerited and therefore hollow. Only in the thought of my father was I a member of the world, one of the masters. He had been a civilian militiaman who had enlisted just before the New Year. Men with any sort of soldiering in their background were rare. He already had two chevrons to go beneath the divisional patch on his arm. For the past ten days, I had lived on the éclat of those bombardier's stripes (he was an anti-aircraft gunner), had felt a kinship with every two-striped soldier I had seen, even with the Americans who wore theirs upside-down.

Three weeks before, in the Sydney Domain, there had been a display aimed at furbishing the confidence of a city faced by invasion. Since I later discovered that my mother's younger brother, who knew the fulfilment of being a sergeant in the infantry, had all of one subaltern above him and all of two Bren gunners beneath him with whom to hold two suburban beachfronts, this display in the Domain was immorally deceptive. Just at the time, it seemed to make the hundreds who looked on bleary-eyed with pride, and at appropriate times, the warm Saturday morning air thudded with applause. Three truck-drawn anti-aircraft guns careered across the park. On spots marked with lime, as for lawn tennis, they jumped to a halt. From the backs of the trucks poured men in scrubbed webbing and battle order. Some of them set up a screen of Bren guns around the gun positions, jamming in the magazines and tugging in a frenzy at the cocking handles. Behind each truck the crews unhooked their guns, unlimbered them, hauled out the extra limbs which stabilised the gun platforms. Intoning formulae like a horde of frantic monks, they climbed or circulated around the trim altars out of which the blunt barrels grew. Through the horizon and dome of space which they commanded, the guns elevated and traversed in unison. This was for me the embarrassing part of the display. Despite their sleekness, they could have been a string of ancient chorus girls, each flinging one graceless leg into the air. Finally, the barrels lowered towards an imaginary sea to shell an imaginary submarine. Then the men began to limber their guns and package them in their covers. Every soldier in the display was an NCO — no mere gunners allowed. Taking up action stations to

14

the rear of the trucks, they numbered off, reported *gun clear, sir*, and saluted the flag. People cheered.

No. 2 on one of the guns was my father, flesh of my flesh, bone of my bone, spinning that barrel and aiming it into the sky by the slightest pressure of his fingers on the controls. Besides which, there were only five such guns in Australia.

There was no doubt that Saturday morning. The Jordans had, to their surprise, joined the masters.

3

It was the Wednesday before Easter. The autumn gales, which used to bring regular floods when we lived on the North Coast, had just struck Sydney. Beneath their violence, the Mantles' place slumped more noticeably into an earth which crawled with rain as if with some sort of organic corruption. From our front bedroom window where I waited to see any stray act of God — a roof blown off, a fence beaten down, a flood at the end of the street — I could survey the flooded approaches of the railway bridge. Earlier that morning, when the local girls, dressed and made up for work, had to take off their shoes and wade to the stairs, there had been some excitement. Now no one came or went except the postman, and I could see, from the way my mother straightened up from gazing into the letter box, that for us his coming and going had produced no result.

She came back into the house and went to the bathroom to hang up the oilskin and dry her hair with a towel. From the slightly opened bathroom window, I could see a little of the Mantles' lighted lounge-room window behind which Lennie and Joseph enjoyed the storm in companionship.

"There's nothing in the box but a big bull-frog," she smiled. I leant my head on her hip and hung my arm about her thighs.

"Never mind," I said.

The vista of sub-tropical rain, falling like blindness over a railway embankment, excessive, numbing, washed all life out of the morning. The world was plotting again; the voice of the rain was built of the sizzling voices of a million conspirators, who had managed to prevent a letter from my father that morning, and might manage God knew what that afternoon.

What they *did* manage was a little variety. At two o'clock, the rain stopped instantaneously. Winds, forty miles an hour, which was faster than a car, cleared the streets of rain. The three willows on the embankment groaned like pensioners. My mother got out my gumboots and we went to visit the Mantles.

That afternoon, Hilda had been ironing what was dry in the lounge-room full of half-dried clothing. Lennie and Joseph sat on a rug playing an esoteric game of Monopoly with an incomplete set. Their cosiness, with the wind thudding at their windows, gave us back our spirits. The boys welcomed us absent-mindedly and I sat down smiling, to watch them battle for Pall Mall and Marylebone Station. As for my mother and Hilda, they had talk of ironing and damp clothes to kindle to.

But there was some special excitement in the way that Hilda flipped the clothes about on the ironing table, in the vigour with which she dealt with the iron. Inevitably, she began to talk about her secret.

"Did I tell you about the new doctor?" she asked. "Well, he's not new, only it's the first I've heard of him. He's in Macquarie Street. Anyhow, the McCalls — you know them, don't you? — they're three up from the bridge — I'll say their backyard'd be flooded — well, they had a grandson, who got rheumatic fever and was just about a cripple, and this man did wonders for him. I'm saving to take Joseph — I never go to a doctor unless I can plonk the money down in front of him.''

My mother said there was no need to worry about that.

"Yes there is. I can't afford to dress as if I had money, so I'd be too ashamed to ask for an account.'' Hilda held up one of the Comrade's shirts to the light.

"Besides,'' she went on, laying it flat and plying the iron as if she'd been born married, "I'm never sure about what I'll have in the future. I can only depend on what I've got in hand. I shouldn't say that. Lennie's'' — she meant the Comrade — "a good provider, but he's got a cause to finance, and he wouldn't be Lennie if he didn't have the cause. And he's got a weakness for the drink too. But he's a good man really. He lives for the boys and he's really dedicated — to the Future and all that. As far as money's concerned, that's half our problem.''

My mother said nothing, and the wind took her part in the dialogue, butting at the walls, dislodging a rowdy piece of slate from the roof-top. Hilda shook her head over the ironing table.

"Poor old place'll fall apart soon. Anyhow, I can't take Joseph until I've got that three guineas tight in my hand. We've got fifteen quid in the bank of course, but I can't touch that. You've got to leave a little bit in reserve. In case something happens like.''

I saw my mother glance at the mouldering skirting boards, the damp spots on the ceilings, the walls dribbling moisture, the naked fly-blown bulb, Joseph's angular lameness — all this in a second. Her face seemed to say with irrepressible honesty, "God, in *case* something happens!''

18

"You wouldn't tell anyone all this?" Hilda asked quickly.

"Of course I wouldn't!"

"Thanks. Glory, they'll all need new shirts before the winter's out."

It was some time after we were overcoated to leave that the Comrade came home at an hour he was not expected. Someone had knocked so strenuously at the door that the panels creaked. Then the Comrade had come in, helped by an older man with a leathery face in the folds of which large drops of rain glinted. The Comrade carried his coat slung across his shoulders and his injured hand in his good one. Tincture or blood seeped horrendously through the bandages. His lips quivered madly, unable to work together in the making of words. Jagged sound hung from his mouth like icicles.

At last he sat down and managed to smile.

"H — had an ax'dent, Hildie," he ground out.

The older man waggled his head rabidly.

"Wish I was as keen on the cause as Len," he breathed.

Hilda ignored him, kneeling to survey the hand. The Comrade held it by the wrist in front of him. It looked like a parcel he would have preferred to leave on a train seat.

"Len, you didn't!" Hilda murmured.

"Brave as the day's long," the old man butted in. "They're having a Holy Thursday protest and want someone to give out the literature. So Len ups with a cleaver and whops into his hand. God, he cut down deep. Look, I think he missed his aim a bit, Mrs Mantle. Of course, as far as *they* know" (he thumbed over his right shoulder towards a *they* that was obtuseness and cruelty in a white coat) "it's accidental like last time.

You don't have to worry. He's got a week off on Compo."

Lennie, Joseph and myself jumped, my mother looked at the floor, when Hilda stood up and whelted the old man across the mouth.

"What in the hell's use is Compo to me? What in the *hell's* use? I've got a cripple of a boy here waiting to go to the doctor. And you offer me Compo as if it were the bloody temple of Solomon." She bunched her right fist against her forehead and began to cry.

"You encourage him," she accused the old man, "to hack away at himself until he's stitches and scars from head to foot. All to hand out dodgers and foul little pieces of paper that don't do a bit of good. You encourage him, but you don't give him anything to make up the difference between Compo and wages! You never do that. You stinking old cesspit of a man."

The old fellow coughed. "Well, I apparently don't get much thanks."

"I'll say you don't!" she hissed. "I'll say you don't. Your wife dresses better than me. You've got lampshades and curtains. You'll never give a drop of your own blood. What a fool Len is! To try and build a perfect world when there'll always be old pharisees like you."

"Go easy, girl," the Comrade managed to say. It was hard to let your eyes leave him. In my mind, shocking ideas on how he got his red handkerchief were galvanising.

"Go home!" Hilda whispered to the old man. "Please! Get going!"

You could see she would try to beat him to a mash if he didn't obey.

"Got to go now, old cock," he called quickly to the Comrade. "Look after yourself. Afternoon."

"You know where the front door is," Hilda prompted; and he showed that he did by slamming it behind him.

Still the Comrade shivered in ecstasy of shock and cold. Bending over him again, Hilda laid her lips on his forehead.

"It's that Doctor Burnett," she said. "He knows what goes on and he never gives Len any pain-killer. As if it should matter to a doctor how a man gets hurt, just as long as he's hurt."

At the mention of the word "Burnett", Comrade Lenin gave a small giggle of reflex pain, pain remembered.

"Look, Mrs Jordan," Hilda called, without turning from her husband, "I haven't any brandy in the house. But he needs . . . Do you think you could . . . ?"

"Yes," my mother said. "I've got a bit inside. Daniel, you can stay here."

With my mother gone, the boys and I tended to drift in closer to the mystery of the Comrade's blood. Hilda hardly saw us. But the Comrade himself noticed our edging and shuffling. He gazed at us exultantly, eyes distended with opiate pain, yet brighter on the borders of shock than they would ever be in states of undistracted normality.

"Do you Theists," he asked me, and you could tell he didn't give a damn whether I knew what a Theist was, "ever suffer like this any more, for what you believe?"

But when my mother brought back the brandy, he drank it as well as any Theist ever did.

4

Lennie Mantle and I saw Joseph as a tithe reserved for death. He merited reverence, for there was something holy about the death of the very young. He was a designated human. The women marked with white crosses in newspaper photographs of crowds were illustrious and lifted out of the masses and designated for £2 by the soap company who ran the whole thing. In a better way than this, Joseph was illustrious and lifted out of the mass. Nor did death present for him any mental block. Hilda had decanted the fear of it from his mind but left its mystery; and I believe that when Comrade Lenin was away at night, and Joseph sobbed with the pain in his limbs, she simply took him in her stout arms and promised him an immortality something like the type Stanislaus believed in, but not the Comrade.

The doomed child Joseph therefore saw himself as a sacramental personage to whom apt concessions were due. He brought games to an end on the basis of his vitiated muscles; imminent death was the first claim he dragged into any dispute.

"You'll only go to Limbo anyhow," I told him, sure of my dogma.

We were lolling in the thick excited sunlight of a Saturday morning. Wartime cars, grunting beneath their bags of gas, drew our lazy eyes; long goods trains set us counting rolling stock. "The Charge of the Light Brigade" was on at the *Mercury*, and girls with their hair crimped inside scarves slip-slopped past to make a reservation for the night session.

"What's Limbo?" Lennie asked. It was a joy to pay them back for their *Soviets* and *Sickles*, their *people's blood*, their *red flags*, *Comin terms* and *catilists*.

"It's where you go if you're not baptised but still young — haven't reached the age of reason. Of course," I conceded lightly to Joseph, "you'll be perfectly happy. You just won't see God."

"Oh, I want to see God," Joseph murmured.

"But there's no God!" said Lennie. His small face was austere and pitying. "How many times has Comrade Lenin got to tell you there's no God?"

Joseph pumped his shoulders up and down. They were like the shoulders of a hawk.

"Hilda told me there is. She says Comrade Lenin just pretends, that it's just part of his politics. It's part of his game."

"If he was only mucking about," Lennie hissed in scandalised certainty, "he would have told me."

A local girl went clipping by long-leggedly, our eyes leaving the dumpy sedans and following her lanky elegance.

"Is Heaven better than Limbo?" Joseph asked, like a fancier buying horses.

"It's much better. You've got perfect happiness, for one thing, and you live like a son of God, which is even better than living like a son of the King."

"Comrade Lenin," Lennie said loudly, "reckons the king's just a lazy old German."

Suddenly Lennie could no longer be suffered. The brat would believe in nothing. He squealed as I sprang on him, sat on his chest, clamped his wrists to the lawn and forced my knee up under his jaw to shut his infidel mouth.

"I bet you want Joseph to be a son of God!" I spat; and when he grunted negatively, I began to twist his left wrist. "Go on. I bet you do!" He began to pale, to nod his head frenziedly. Having been told by Eucheria that you cannot hurry the things of God, that part of the work must be left to grace, I dismounted from Lennie's unregenerate pot-belly.

"But you'd have to be baptised," I explained, turning back to Joseph.

Even then, it seemed that there was a speculate light kindled in Joseph's eye. "If you've got to be baptised," the light said, "I'll have five bob of that."

"How do you get baptised?" he asked.

"Don't think I won't tell Comrade Lenin," Lennie told his brother.

Joseph's long white arm reached to the back of Lennie's head and clipped it vigorously, sending Lennie hiccuping with sobs to the veranda corner where he draped himself with dramatic feeling against the cold brick.

"It's easy," I pursued. "I'd just pour water over your head, all the time saying, 'I baptise thee in the name of the Father and of the Son and of the Holy Ghost. Amen.' "

As if he were afraid of catching a cold beneath those vivifying waters, Joseph squinted up at the sun.

"How much water?"

"A cupful would do it. I'll get Lennie."

"Why?"

"He'll have to be your godparent."

24

"*Godparent?*" Joseph stared at his brother, looking for some secret dignity hitherto unknown.

"Oh, it just means someone who becomes the mother or father of your soul. It's not particularly important."

"But why?"

"That's the way we do things."

Wanting to spread peace in readiness for the Sacrament, I strolled up to the veranda corner to trap Lennie's goodwill with a barrel of honey. He was slumped, choking on tearless grief. I put my hand on his shoulder and he couldn't have shuddered more if I'd touched something flayed.

"Are you all right, Lennie? Do you want to come and see Joseph get baptised?"

Lennie screamed and kicked sideways.

"I'll belt hell out of you if you do that again, Mantle. Now come on, we need a godparent if we can get one. You can be godparent if you like."

"Don't think I won't tell Comrade Lenin!"

"I'm not scared of damned Comrade Lenin."

As Joseph and I went off for a bowl of water, and Lennie looked after us with uncontrollable interest, I regretted that the rite I was to perform lacked greater mystery. Yet mystery enough it had to draw Lennie. I was involved with Joseph in an Inquisition of Faith behind the garage when Lennie limped along to give grudging witness to the making of a Christian.

"Do you believe all the Catholic truths, Joseph?"

"What's a Catholic truth?"

I sighed. "Do you believe Christ is God?"

"The boy in the Christmas Hymns?"

"Yes."

"All right. I believe in him."

I paused with the bowl of water in my hands. Could it be as easy as this to send a man to paradise?

"Ready, Lennie?" I asked inconsequentially.

I doused Joseph Stalin Mantle's head and washed him newborn in the name of the Trinity. The heavens did not open up to receive him.

When an American troop-train hove along the outside line at processional pace, the baptismal waters hadn't dried on Joseph's head. From where we stood, we couldn't see the railway for brick garages, but Lennie pointed across country to the street corner where three girls waved in that unique gay manner kept for US personnel. The men in the troop-train were barracking back inimitably. The way they roused a suburban street was also unique.

We swept into the road in time to be seen by the Americans. They seemed to hang from the windows eight at a time. Crisp-shirted, white-toothed, overpaid, flushed with illegal spirits brewed in Woolloomooloo backyards, when they saw us they flung handfuls of His Majesty's coin into the street. There was time to be grateful, to stand in the pinging rain and wave for a second before turning to booty. In that urbane second, from every angle, the railway bridge, the corners, the lanes, ran flurries of children who had heard and recognised the noise of the Yanks coming up the Western line. The leisurely glut, the immense spoils, half-vanished before we could turn to the interlopers. Slower, smaller, fatter children came, grubbing for coin in the gutter, along the embankment fence, on the roadway. There was only a pittance left for us.

Joseph and I *did* see a sleek florin land in the mud below the embankment, but he was still very fast on his spidery legs. Though I pinned him to the dirt, sat across his body, hammered his stomach, he reminded me that he was a new-made saint — if I'd believed what I'd said.

26

He got up from the dirt with that limitlessly negotiable two shillings in his suety hand, and limped across the street in the stilted way his disease imposed on him.

A boy ran past me waving sticks of American gum in my face, that fabled gum whose very wrappings were cherished and gave prestige to their owners. But for my manners, such as they were, it could have been mine.

"You can go to — hell!" I called after him, but he dashed away in his aureole of good fortune which wasn't pierced by the kick I aimed at his backside.

Anyhow, I had done the work of the Lord that morning.

5

I think it was my father's last leave, and we spent the
Sunday afternoon watching the Rugby League at
Calwell Park. It was a sensible way to use up the last
clumsy hours, for we were a family whom, at the best of
times, idleness half-killed with melancholy.

There was an ill-controlled rout in the "A" grade at
the Park that day, and Abattoirs United, a team of
mighty slaughtermen, reduced the enemy in the first
half. It was five minutes before half-time that inspira-
tion died as if by mass consent. The crowd's voice went
drab; we could all have been people watching a
demonstration of cleaning fluid or margarine; the
sublime hysteria was gone. They became an imposition
on us then, all those others, cluttering the time of
farewell with stale talk, stirring the lees of evaporated
frenzy, pulling their cardigans about them, hitching
their cuffless wartime trousers. My father asked if we'd
like to go home.

There had been a volcano erupting, everyone knew,
on a Japanese-held island in the north. This was why the
sunsets were the colour of rust and the afternoon light
so bronze. It lay bronze now across the lawns in the

reserve outside the Park. It turned to stiff copper the high up leaves of the blue-gums where, the Mantles said, koalas had once lived. It dashed tawny on us from amongst the grey trunks, and nuzzled the brown flanks of shrubs. It gave the lie to the Andrews sisters who were being pumped through the loudspeakers inside the Park, chortling "The Best Things in Life Are Free". We were not its masters, my father even was not its master. Definitively, and not without deep shock, I saw him as much a visitor to the earth as I was, saw the heavy tunic rasping the reddened neck, rubbing away at a crease in the flesh. On the palms of my hands, a sweat of love sprang out.

Comrade Lenin was at a meeting at the Domain that afternoon; we had come across him once in there, handing out handbills, yearning to be called up to the platform to speak. Hilda told us they were training him as an orator, but that it took a long time. In any case, on the strength of the man's absence, I was allowed next door.

It was not too late nor too cold to play *Scorched Earth*, their new game, in the tall yellow grass. This was a confused and riotous form of battle, in which sometimes we would snipe in unison at an enemy advancing from the direction of the Mantles' lavatory, and sometimes we would stalk each other amongst the rank spears of paspalum, sweating, worming, outflanking.

I can remember crawling along the verge of the heavier grass in deep shadow when Comrade Lenin's kick took me at the base of the spine and pitched me into a tousle of buffalo grass that had been three feet away. It didn't particularly hurt to be kicked in that way, it was the unadorned violence that outraged a person. I knew, even before I saw him, that only the Comrade, amongst all people I knew, could see clear to shame me so completely in front of Joseph and Lennie. Their shocked and overheated faces swam now above the tangle of grasses like two ash-grey, daytime moons.

"And while I was playing *his* bloody game!" I thought. "Comrade almighty Lenin's almighty game!"

"Look at the little Messiah!" he smiled, very genially. He'd been drinking sabbath sly grog in the back of some fruitshop; and he smelt of the over-ripeness of fruit, the woodiness of packing cases, as well as of illegal liquor. Altogether it seemed that kicking a child hard below the spine was the Comrade's idea of climaxing an elegant afternoon.

"Did anyone ask you to go soul-saving?"

By now I had crawled to my feet. The blunt feel of the Comrade's boot remained, the impact seemed to be fixed in my flesh like a beam of wood. Now I even glanced at his putty eyes, driven to it by the dignity of being right, the immensity of the outrage.

"You're a narrow-chested little runt," he remarked. "But you've certainly got a skinful of all sorts of dogmatics and lies. And you go round spewing them all over my boys."

He had said all this as dispassionately as a judge, but now he grabbed my shoulders and began shaking me.

"Don't you think," he groaned, "that it's bad enough the poor little bastard's a cripple without you baptising him?"

Then he let me go, hiccuped with grief, bit his lip, tears racing down either side of a spongy nose. There was a moisture which was sweat or dribble or tears amongst the bristles of his upper lip.

"Am I supposed to be tickled pink? Joseph's lame, Alleluia? Am I supposed to put up with a little cow like you running round, slopping water over him?"

He began to sway from the waist with grief and anger, which reminded me of the Saturday night two years before in the north when Eve Mulcahy's fiancé had been killed, his truck having stalled straddling the railway line just as the North Coast Mail came galloping up through the dusk. He'd died fiddling with the choke, said one of my uncles who was a shunter. But when my father went in to tell Eve, talcumed and in her slip, getting ready for the dead man to arrive, she had swayed, superbly young white arms raised to her temples, monumentally grieved, just as the Comrade, different creature though he was, quaked with grief now. I expected him, like Eve, to begin keening at any second.

Instead, he clouted me on the right cheek as well as, in his awry state, he could. Too mighty a blow to hurt, it swung me back down to his unkempt lawn. A sound of frying filled the shell of my head. For a long time nothing, sound nor sight, pierced the wadding of numbness that swathed my senses. Then what I heard first was Hilda calling to the boys.

"Joseph, Lennie! Come inside!"

The authoritativeness of hysteria sharpened her voice, and the boys, who'd been standing petrified up to now waist-deep in grass, moved to her, their gaping white faces passing me as I tried to stand up.

"Hurry!" Hilda screamed to them. Before the stridency of the word had ceased thrumming the darkening air, before the people at the dozen kitchen windows around were aware of him, my father came running out of the Mantles' lane.

He was much shorter, much solider than the Comrade. His face was neat and brown from the sun and temporary fury. He had spent weeks at some jungle-training place where they taught you to throw Japs on their backs, so that the sodden Comrade was scarcely a

31

challenge to him. The people in the windows, hoping to see the living daylights thrashed out of the Comrade, must have laughed cruelly when they saw him arrive. Hilda must have scolded the boys away from the kitchen windows and dragged them into the lounge whence they couldn't see into the yard.

Perhaps it was gratitude that finally turned my stomach over as I reeled to the fence and was sick.

My father was facing the Comrade, looking up into his eyes. A few vague syllables bubbled on his lips before he lashed out at the over-rich lips, the wide, porous nose, the eyebrows hanging like dewlaps. He was terribly merciless, dragging up off the ground again and again a Comrade who in his turn was terribly unresistant. Soon the Comrade was choking on blood, spilling it down his chin as my father stood back to regain breath.

"Come on, you bastard," the Comrade growled thickly through clogged lips. "Wallop hell out of me. Maybe you can make me believe in a God who makes cripples out of little children."

My father pointed to him and said, coolly enough, "Don't try to make yourself into a bloody atheist martyr, Mantle. You're just scum that tried to bash up a child ten minutes ago."

The Comrade sagged to the ground, grunted, sighed, shrugged. My mother had arrived, crying without a sound, and was lifting me up. As she cupped my head into her shoulder blade, I released my own tears softly, and in them dissolved the entire shock of the incident. A little retching, a few tears had restored me.

"Come on, Brian! Come home now," she begged hoarsely.

Hunched on the ground, his long black Chinese hair falling forward in his eyes, the Comrade didn't move.

"Call it a day?" She persisted softly, but as with Hilda earlier the few words were barbed with a kind of hysteria, and hysteria was something my father, as well as Lennie and Joseph, was in terror of.

"If you go near Stell or Daniel again, I'll kill you," he said quickly to the Comrade. "Or if not me, then her father. Or her brother. If you drive her to leave next door, I'll see to it you never get a second's peace till they bury you."

Still the Comrade didn't move, humped on the ground, a formless organism capable of taking in boundless pain.

"I'll send you back to the slime you rose from," my father reiterated. "Do you understand?"

The Comrade said nothing.

So we collected ourselves and went home to tea.

6

It is easy to remember the two distinct armies who mustered on the steam level of Central railway on an autumn night in 1942. There were those who had no families in that city; for whom the shattering business of farewell was over; who could clown by the indicator, buy *Smith's Weekly* at the news-stall, champ down a last pie. For these were the things the excitement of what was merely a train trip provoked you to.

Closer in towards the barrier a more orderly brand of soldier gathered, standing in tight family knots where everyone's eyes were too bright, everyone's laughter too brittle and reverent. Women spoke up shrilly, nursing their duty not to begin weeping at least until the order to board rang out. As if the shelling and privation would begin the moment their train cleared the point which read, "Unauthorised persons . . .", etc., every man wore webbing and gaiters, waterbottle and rifle. This gave them the look of being soldiers forever, of having taken vows for life in some dubious brotherhood. It made them solemnly gallant for their last moments with their people; but when flurries of steam rose scaldingly from the underbelly of the engine, turning people's heads, the faces above the webbing and accoutrements were drained pale for a second or two.

The train lay empty along the station length; skin-tight with light, waterbottles dusted and full for the trip to the coast. The upholstery was dull and tidy. It was perhaps the cleanest train I have ever seen. But in all its virgin cleanliness, it served merely to emphasise departure. God knew to how many wives and mothers those clean yellow lights were themselves only a leer and a threat.

My father brought us to a stop outside the barrier. In the lee of the indicator we hid, as if we could thus beguile the mechanisms of war, lull the efficiency of battery commanders, render forgetful the train seething beyond the gate.

"Well, plenty of good time!" my mother said. If gaiety were some sort of fever, a rising line on a graph beyond the crest of which were tears, then you could have claimed that she was gay.

"Here comes my troop commander," my father muttered to her and, as a young officer went by smiling at them, they grinned back strainedly, a glib lie of a smile which gave no light to the wide misery in their eyes, and died on their lips the instant the lieutenant had passed.

"Right at this moment," said my father through clamped teeth, "I could kill that bastard Nicholson."

"That's a flattering thought," Stell smiled. "You're leaving us, and all you can think of is Nicholson." She had reached out and was touching his tunic'd elbow. Perhaps a nerve was there by which he could be soothed.

"But it isn't right, Stell. I could maybe have gotten out of this. That's the thing I won't forget. How in the hell you can forgive me, Stell, is more than I can understand."

"What about the *kill-me-deads*?" she insisted, pressing a little biscuit tin into his hands. It was full of *kill-me-deads*, which were his name for small fruit cakes.

"I won't forget them." He stamped his boot on the tarred floor, not hard enough though to make his private anguish public. "I just had to go to Nicholson and make application. If I had, I might have been allowed to stay with you. Till after Herbie came anyway." For ten seconds he was quiet. His eyelids seemed to swell and dip in honour of our pitifulness. *Herbie* was his name for his unborn child. He was a great man for names and codes. "I honestly don't think I would have got away with it, Stell. But I should have tried it. That's where I let you down, girl."

"I didn't expect you to make any application." There was a scolding, bright humorousness in her eyes which might soon become unfunny in the extreme. "I don't want to hear the word again. There are other things to talk about than pink forms in triplicate. Surely there are! Life is more than the filling-out of forms, though that's what they're trying to reduce it to."

"I'm sorry for the language, Danny boy," he nodded to me. "But it's hard to leave the two of you on the one night without swearing."

Someone blew a whistle blast that cut off all our breaths.

"That's not for me," my father reassured us.

My mother frowned. "The thing to do," she said, "is to forget all this business about applications and Nicholson."

"Stell, you should have seen the way he treated the other poor bloke who tried to apply."

Stell hung her head and bit her lower lip. He took her by the elbows — it was too early yet for a more desperate gesture.

"I'm sorry," he said. "I can't help harping on it. It's all I can think of, now that I'm going."

"Well, I don't want another word," she decreed in a clear, angry, level, absolving tone. "When you come home, you'll laugh about men like Nicholson. You'll laugh and toss Herbie on your knee."

Air Force men who had been summoned by the whistle began to move through the barrier, flanked by women who, besides a few hysterically gay, were erect and pallid, or sobbing and chewing their grief into their handkerchiefs.

"Why are they crying?" I asked.

"Those men are mainly airgunners. A lot of them get killed, Danny. That's all there is to it."

The sling of his rifle had been galling his shoulder and he was tired of it. He dropped the butt on the floor with an unmilitary clatter belying the stripes on his arms. Then he forced a slow, but in the end, authentic smile.

"I'm not very brave," he said. "I'm the least brave of the three of us. It's the truth, what you've said, Stell. It's a matter of here we are. We have to live on from here. Look, Stell!"

I could see, in his eyes beneath the substantial shade of the slouch hat, two fierce little squares of light, the reflection of the lights of the station without, but also of a sudden zest within. For, all his life, he shuttled between the utmost borders of fatalism, where all a man could do was comment on his own destiny, and some central temperate zone where the human personality shone unassailably, and the human will rose to heaven like a fortress. Like some angel, he travelled at the speed of light between the two climes, knowing no middle latitudes, dwelling only where either courage or abandonment to the flux of things was the ultimate intelligent virtue. During his time, he practised more than his share of both. But that's another story.

"Never be lonely, Stell," he persuaded my mother. "They can't take a man away just by putting him on a damned train and trying to." The big hat nodded reverently. "Thank God, I believe in the bloody soul of man. Loneliness is only a feeling. It's what we eat for breakfast. Let's both refuse to tolerate it, Stell."

He looked down at me and I couldn't help catching the furious excitement in his face. Though he knew as I knew that when the train cleared Central, he would be vanished and lost to us, he seemed to have half-baffled himself, and to be yearning to get aboard and find out for good if loneliness *was* simply what he'd had for breakfast.

"And don't you ever be afraid, Danny boy. Especially not of mongrels like the Comrade. If the sky falls in, it doesn't alter the fact. I'm your father and you're my son. For eternity. Do you know what eternity is?"

Eucheria had told me. "For ever and ever."

"I'll say!" he said. "I'll think of you all the time. We'll never really lose each other."

But then the bugle began, cackling high over the fruit stalls and refreshment rooms, flushing pigeons out of the sooty dome eighty feet above our heads. He paled, as if already, in the eighth second of eternity, we *were* lost to each other. My mother took him, webbing and rifle too, into her arms. For a second, his forehead came down and, with the brim of his hat pushed back unregimentally, rested on her shoulder.

"Just think of what it'll be like to come home," she whispered. "Do you really think you let us down? Just see the way some of these other fellows let their people down, what with booze and gambling and women."

He lifted his head and frankly crushed her against the

38

unlovely basic pouches which cluttered his chest. They held each other as courting couples do, and made as frantic a leave-taking as any of the desperate couples embracing beneath the great roof.

Already half the regiment was through the barrier. He opened his arms widely enough to take three boys my size, and enclosed me. His webbing crushed my ribs. A few seconds, and he rose, his eye half-taken by the mass of khaki soldiery lunging past the ticket box.

"Got to go, Stell," he explained. "Live well. You'll be getting most of the pay. No booze and gambling and women for me. And if anyone gives you trouble, just go back to old Finnie" (old Finnie being an ancestral god who claimed to be my grandfather). "And God help anyone who gives you trouble then!"

He went and pushed through the barrier with some obscure urgency. On the platform, around the clumps of gunners, battery sergeant-majors, superb, beefy creatures who had apparently no origins, no wives, no issue, strode around calling, "Five minute area, M battery." "Fall in K battery!" Until the clots of uniforms dissolved and formed a sudden pattern, and a whole regiment was drawn up on the asphalt beside its train. The extravagant noises of the sar-majors had quietened those watching from behind the barrier wire, those whose only claim on the men beyond were the futile ones of blood or eternal love. The RSM, against the sole noise of a snuffling steam engine, gave over the parade to Lieutenant-Colonel Nicholson. He was an alien-looking little man, this officer so tolerant of applications for compassionate leave; alien with his weathered, brandy-nobbling grazier's face and his thin moustache the colour of cotton-bush.

Through the grille, we could no longer see my father, already lost somewhere in M battery, all fear, all

39

love, all curses against Nicholson tucked neatly into his tunic and his face unnaturally bland.

I didn't sit still in the train roaring us back to our empty suburb. The pathos of my lonely father set me writhing into the leather of the seat, writhing against my mother's side. There was disapproval on the part of each conscious adult in the carriage. There were a number of unconscious ones — lovers slumped deathly at the end of the corridor, three or four middle-aged men napping in their seats, sated, older than the world, not simply dead but breathing on in the nth degree of death. A barrel-chested matron sat up like the wife of Mammon, watching and disliking me. It was an evil night.

When we left the train, a nor'-westerly drove a sharp drizzle into our eyes. I put my face into my mother's hip, against the sight of our street slimy with a compound of sump oil and dew of death, against the long gleam of the eight lines sweeping away to other dead towns.

My mother asked if I'd like cocoa when we got home. I said, oh boy I would, just like a boy in the pictures said it.

"As long as it doesn't keep you awake," she cautioned.

"No. You wait and see."

Sleep would be no trouble. In its dark hours, the frazzled pod of the earth would split and a new world spill out. The prospect did not excite, but it managed to provoke a drowsy interest in what might result.

7

"The sunsets are blood-red," Aunt Verna told me. "Blood-red with the blood of poor soldiers!"

After a russet winter's day, the sunsets had a right to be blood-red. But the grind of the seasons had little meaning for Aunt Verna beside the drama of the times, the war news, the mashed and bayoneted deaths being died just over the northern horizons. The newspaper tucked high under her left arm, close to her fierce heart, she clutched the door knob, whispered, "I don't think the little yellow beasts will get here," and opened the door. There was a job waiting for her in Queensland and she feared to take it.

Behind the door, drawn up to the set table, sat my uncle, he who had the holding of two beaches on his mind. He turned his darkling face to us and smiled his crooked piratical smile. In his eyes was no concern for all that indefensible space which was his to defend. To me he seemed *the* buccaneer, ageless, deathless, of endless resource, fit to stand on the battlefields of the world with Errol Flynn, and match him miracle for miracle.

"G'day Tiger!" he laughed, shaping up for a fight. I

came at him swinging punches, landing them on his khaki arms.

"Hey, wait there, Tiger!" he roared, and holding both my wrists with his right hand, he pulled from his pocket a honeycomb bar available only to HM Forces, a treasure, though soggy with body heat. Aunt Verna took it away from me, and before we could start another rough-house, my mother had the meal ready.

Her face was uniformly of a superb pallor since my father had gone. Her brows beneath the hair-line were glossy and hard like celluloid. The swathe of brown hair swaying over her shoulders somehow added to her air of profound fatigue. Matt rose up to take from her the plates she was carrying. She smiled. There was no doubt, the smile said. She was glad that they were here, that she was entertaining them.

The table talk was a disappointment that night. They were waiting for me to eat up and go, which I did eagerly as the price of hearing something worthwhile. I was permitted to leave and slide away into the back bedroom which I had been sharing with Verna for some weeks. My fort was there, an impregnable little fort of butter-boxes being held successfully by two machine gun crews, left out in the sun last summer and badly contorted, two Royal Household Cavalry with movable lances, a number of kneeling, crouching, grenade-throwing Highlanders, one slouch-hatted Australian, who was my father and commanded the fort, and one Zulu, who was my father's Man Friday. Deployed suicidally in a frontal attack on the place was a haphazard assortment of mercenary elements — three of them headless, most of them lacking paint — and two Germans who were the master spirits of this evil seige, and who would in the end die complex deaths at the hands of my father and the Zulu. But it would be a long battle and ill-fortune would for a long time blunt the arms of the defenders. Not until one of the machine gun crews lay dead beside their weapon, one of the Household Cavalry went down in blood and a flurry of hoofs, and some of the Highlanders fell back with the grenades still in their hands, would my father lead his men down from the fort and drive the enemy from the plain.

I reopened battle casually, making intermittent explosives noises to show those at the table that it was now safe to talk.

"Well," my uncle said, "I've got it, Verna."

"How much do I owe you?" Verna asked.

"It's all right. The bloke concerned owes me a favour. Anyhow, I gave him three bottles."

"Oh, I'll have to pay you for them."

"Don't carry on, Verna! They were issued to us, and I always save my beer issue. In this country, there's no one from a horse trainer down to a Prime Minister you can't bribe with beer."

"So you're going, Verna — definitely?" my mother asked.

"Yes," Verna admitted, ashamed. "But I feel I should be here for — for Herbie, you know. That's what I worry about. After all, I'm not as stupid or as cruel as the — well, we'll call it *confounded* government. But if I leave you now . . ."

"Don't worry about it, Verna. Pat's coming down from the Cape to look after Daniel. You'd be wrong to stay for that reason. Just the same, you *should* stay. For other reasons."

No one spoke for five seconds. There was a soft sound such as a canary makes as it squeaks and mumbles amongst the seed. It was Aunt Verna drinking tea. *The herb that cheers but not inebriates*, it had nevertheless lost Verna her job. A floorwalker at

Tonkin and Watt had found her sipping it in a fitting room one Saturday morning. He and the management had treated the affair as an outrage to the war effort, the future of the country being inextricably involved in the future of Tonkin and Watt's corsetry section.

"It's bad when a trained corsetière can't get work," Verna claimed. "The fall of Singapore did it."

"Not only the fall of Singapore," Matt laughed. "You should see the Yanks scatter those dollars round up in Kings Cross."

"But wages don't go up," Verna said acidly. "No, not wages!"

Wages *didn't* go up. Women skimped on the grace of the human form and spent their money on food. There were vacancies, the corset factories told her, but they were all above the Brisbane line, and if the country was invaded, the Government might abandon the North. There was a job begging in Mackay, a sugar port in the north, offering wages in keeping with a town above an undefended Capricorn. Mackay was a thousand miles away and Verna had no train money.

She finished her cup of tea. "I'll never forget this, Matt," she murmured. "I really will never forget it. I'll never forgive myself for putting you in such danger — a solider who could be sent off to New Guinea and killed at any time."

"Don't go putting curses on me, Verna. There wasn't any danger. The return half of a ticket to Mackay that's never been used; a refund's been paid out on it and it was just lying around the Central ticket office doing no good. My mate only had to pick it up."

"I didn't mean that sort of danger. I mean, I've got you to steal for me. Ten pounds' worth of railway ticket. Grave matter, as the priests say. And I'm supposed to be a Catholic!"

Both Labor people, and bred by old Finnie on a sense of the sacredness of work and protest, my mother and Matt began simultaneously to click their tongues over this scruple of Aunt Verna's. Their God visited the sins of the vested interests only.

"London's being bombed, men are coughing blood in bloody Libya, Russia's in flames. And Verna Jordan thinks God's sitting on her shoulder waiting to see what she's going to do next to offend him. Look, Verna! If he damns anyone, it'll be Tonkin and bloody Watt he damns. Whether you're going or not, keep the ticket. If I was killed tomorrow, I wouldn't want to go to any Heaven they keep you out of for helping your friends."

"Watch out, Matt!" my mother hushed him. "Daniel's got ears like an elephant."

I made more battle noises. The siege sprang alive again, one of the headless mercenaries dying in his own blood on the rim of the drawbridge.

"I wish," Verna said, "I had a robust conscience like you, Matt. You're going to be a lucky catch for some girl or other."

"I'm still hanging around for you to give me the green light, Verna," he called heartily, and the three of them gave a formal chuckle.

Suddenly, out of the tail-end of the laugh, Verna spoke up in bitterness, regardless of me. I let peace fall on my battlefield and raised my head to miss none of her genuine anguish.

"I'm a poor bloody spinster of a woman." She was blaming somebody, but neither my mother nor Matt. "What's a spinster without her job? A little bit of nothing, done up in a black dress and grinning all damn day behind a counter at the best of times. Without the black dress and the counter, she might as well not even exist. And to get a job I have to commit a crime and be the only poor bloody Australian advancing to meet the Japs.''

"That settles it, Verna,'' my mother said. A chair groaned. She must have been standing over Verna now. "We can't let you go.''

"I've got to. A poor spinster's her job. Jobless, she may as well be dead. If the Japs are two miles outside Mackay when I get there, still I'll take the job.''

"Don't make a drama of it, Verna,'' my mother persisted with suspect strength of nerve. "You aren't just *any poor bloody old spinster who may as well be dead.* Not to us.''

Verna sniffed loudly. When she spoke, her voice had a shaky resonance which came of being close to tears.

"The ticket's been stolen.'' She laid her tongue down very heavily on each accent. "I'll have to go now. I can't put Matt to all that trouble without using the ticket.''

"Verna!'' said Matt airily. "It *was* no trouble. I am not sitting in the maw of hell, and the army doctors assure me I'm not possessed of devils. See! And finally, I wouldn't go to Mackay with a whole bloody division of tanks.''

"Since I've got to go anyway,'' Verna asked quietly, "why don't you make the whole thing easier for me? All this pressure on me —''

"I'm sorry, Verna. You're a good woman. Really you are. This is not a brat of a soldier talking now. You're a good woman, so I suppose you'll get looked after. I'll tell you what though. It'll be God or the Yanks who save you, because that part of the country can't be held.''

"Well, don't any of you worry,'' Verna all but whispered, and still I was hearing her, I thought in triumph. "I'll kill myself gladly, joyfully, before any of those little yellow things get their hands on me.''

Then there was silence, such a long one that I became

46

self-conscious about the battle and forgot it. Perhaps the three of them had died in their chairs at table. I rushed out to them, holding my breath, but of course they were all there, Verna and Matt sitting up, my mother slumped, a figure of grief which I did not wish to jolt into tears. It was for her husband sleeping in a transit-camp in Egypt, for her intransigent sister-in-law, for her born and unborn sons that she sat peering down into the black mine of her unmilked tea.

I was still awake, listening for trains, when Verna came to my bedside to attend to my window and perhaps start yarning. Now that the ticket to Mackay was in her hand-bag, torturous farewell threatened. She crouched over me in time to see my eyes snap shut too vigorously.

"Daniel!"

"Yes?"

"You haven't made your First Communion yet?"

"No."

"You haven't got a sin on your soul?"

"No." It was the theologically based opinion of Eucheria, though I had doubts on the question.

"You'll have to remember your poor Aunt Verna. Especially if anything happens to her."

"Yes."

"You'll have to remember me always. Till you're an old man. You'll have to pray for my soul. Will you?"

"Yes."

"Always?"

"Yes."

"Promise?"

"Yes."

"That's the boy."

She stood upright, gazed down at my body, taut with embarrassment, and sighed in the face of the future.

47

Around the room she moved, picking up a toothbrush, plucking her nightgown from beneath the pillow, fumbling for her vanishing cream in her handbag. As she went out, I thought, "I'm glad I'm not alone like that." By the time she had finished in the bathroom, I was asleep.

Verna could not have been further north than Rockhampton when a Federal Minister announced a marvellous victory in the Coral Sea. The land, the continent, was saved. Eucheria lined us up and took us past the black hole, up the aisle to the sanctuary, to thank the God of triumphs.

8

In the case of the Comrade, one never knew when you would spin round to find him gazing at you. For the Comrade followed out no orbit. A cloven bloody hand, a lightning strike, Party business, even release from Clarence Street lock-up after one of his bad nights; any of these could land him quietly in the corner of one's vision. Such an advent was a peril against which I said a prayer nightly. Yet every month or so, it would happen; and neither the dreamy dislike in his eye nor the vague mockery hanging like lichens on his big lips disturbed me half as much as his sharp interest in me, his clear desire to enter into my mind.

From the cover of their gas meter casing, Joseph and Lennie had me pinned down behind my brick fence by a tempest of fire. There was a bullet in my shoulder. Elegant cords of blood hung like campaign ribbons from the wound. But the essential thing was to be Gene Autry, an honour given according to a rough sort of roster and as the result of an elemental form of collective bargaining. That Friday afternoon, I was Gene Autry and would take many another flesh wound before worming up to the gas box and persuading the two of them to die. Persuasion was necessary. Both of them were liable to lose their dramatic integrity, and while a person performed epics of valour as Gene Autry, they could never be trusted not to turn into some other giant of the West.

In the shade of the wide brick gate post, I lay close for a second, favouring my shoulder wound, ramming .45 calibre cartridges into the heel of my hand. As I rolled over to fire from the unexpected side of the post, my eyes swept through an arc containing keen blue sky and cirrus-cloud, railway stanchion and the dead-fish eyes of Comrade Lenin, who stood on the footpath as still as a totem. An electric train galloped past, stampeded across the viaduct. By the time it had pounded itself away down the western line, Joseph and Lennie had raced to the Comrade. I stood close to the post and watched a caterpillar unfurl itself along a channel of mortar.

It was Friday afternoon, pay afternoon, and scarcely more than a quarter past four. Yet he seemed to be already something more than half-drunk, which promised a bad weekend for Hilda. Though the lines of his face were soggy, just a little more abstinence and a good shave could have had him looking Messianic. It was a debased air of prophetism which kept the boys subject to his word, loyal to his ideas. To that extent he was a good dialectical materialist, in that to his offspring he seemed to be not a continuous personality but a series of projections; they seemed to be able to believe in him as the seer of this particular hour rather than as the violent drunk of last week, the absentee father of last night.

Now, with his boys beside him, without warning, that flush of rapture he'd shown the afternoon he'd butchered his own hand lit up his cheeks. Today there was no shuddering with ecstacy and pain, but the excitement in his eyes was almost as frightening.

"I could really show you boys something," he intoned.

"What is it, Comrade?" Lennie asked, but the Comrade looked up and down the railway line, not wanting to shout above the rush of a train.

"We're the blokes who've got the power," he whispered after a while, "the *real* power!"

He spat into a handkerchief, staring at me. Then for a time he inspected the spit, perhaps, like old Finnie's sister who seemed to get a lot of sinus, desiring the mucous to be a definite colour.

"It'd be a lesson to you boys," he said. "It'd be a better education than anything you've had crammed in so far."

We did not move, the boys and I; we did not dispute this view on education. But the Comrade was undecided.

"Damn it," he belched, abandoning himself utterly to his pay-day excitement; to the excitement of sunshine on the embankment, and a roseate gutful of liquor; to the excitement, above all else, of having a momentous secret for the first and last time in his life, and of convincing us that for him such secrets were routine.

"But you'll have to promise to keep quiet about this," he said, and I realised that he was indeed drunk, expecting Lennie to keep a secret.

"I promise, Comrade," Lennie whispered, making an extravagant X across his chest, wishing his heart, liver and various other organs ripped out if he ever said a word.

"What about you, especially," the Comrade glowered at me. "Will you promise by Christ or the Virgin Mary or somebody?"

He mumbled the names as if they were from an electoral roll, which provoked me to look straight into those shallow swamps of eyes and repeat the formula Eucheria had taught us for moments when someone like the Comrade demanded a solemn pledge.

"I promise, as I fear God and honour the King."

"Well, bugger me!" the Comrade shrugged. "That'll have to do me, I s'pose."

You could see that he was a master of some crafts when he turned away, and this time hawked a gob of spittle from his mouth, lofting it into the wind so that it lobbed itself, with a delicacy of a kind, into the gutter.

"Well, come on!" he said.

He led us to the corner a few blocks away which had a tiny, well-tended reserve. Amongst a narrow diagonal path, a bird bath, a bubbler, two benches, a holly (far from home!), a rhododendron or two, and a row of camphor laurels, clogged with railway soot one day, washed clean the next by rain, there was hardly room for any human. Around the reserve was a low brick wall. Across the road were brown flats kept by scraggy ladies whose underwear flapped in the world's sight from bits of cord tied across landings. The brick wall stopped the contagious beauty of the laurels from infecting all this. Most people sat here on the wall at some time or other. It was a good place to rest children on your way to the shopping centre, or to sit and read of the cataclysm in Europe while you waited for the pub to open. An old man was sitting there, eyeing a paper with sad wisdom, as we came up.

"Sit here!" said the Comrade, and so we did. He was more than half-way towards sitting down himself before he realised how hard it is for a tall, sozzled man to sit down on a low brick fence. He straightened rakishly, stretched, put both hands on his hips and groaned fraudulently.

"Lumbago," he muttered. "I'll just stand here for a while. They haven't arrived yet anyhow."

"Who?" Lennie asked quickly.

"Blabbermouth!" the Comrade spat in a rich, savage basso. The old man looked along the fence at us as if we were all part of the futility he'd been just now reading about.

"Blabbermouth," the Comrade repeated more serenely.

There was nothing in that irksome roadway, except awe for the Comrade, to keep us seated like young gentlemen at his knee. A weary lady with a moustache bore her weekend meat towards us in her graceless arms as if it were a sick child. At the highway end of the street, the yellow-tiled Glasgow Arms had spilt some of its drinkers out into the afternoon sun. Groups of soldiers and workers pecked at their beer and spat into the gutter at moments of either intense humour or intense disgust. Lennie glanced up at his father's straining face and was clearly thinking of asking him once more what we were to look for, and even more clearly thinking the better of it.

We began to talk and nearly forgot the Comrade's presence. Inconsequential traffic rolled by, and the old man folded his paper and jogged away around the corner, while all the time the Comrade said nothing but looked dubiously towards the highway.

Joseph was speaking on the difference between the Australian and American cowboy. The Australian wore no gunbelt but carried his weapons hidden somewhere, or stuck through the belt which merely kept his trousers up. If he took his revolver out, it rarely went back till it spilt blood. (All this, Hilda's father, a genial old fellow who detested the Comrade, had told him.) He was hell with a stock-whip. He could rip a man's head off with it. He was not . . .

"Be quiet!" the Comrade called out. "Here they come!"

From the highway, three canvas-covered trucks made an entry to the street and parked across from the Glasgow Arms. Nearly army trucks, they lacked the unit flashes above the bumper bars and were driven by civilians. Their shrouded cargoes were a mystery.

"Just watch!" the Comrade advised us urgently, foreseeing questions. "Watch the men who get down out of those trucks," he told us, and we studied them as they cuffed the cabin doors closed with that giant-biting-a-biscuit crunch and strolled towards the pub. But there was nothing of consequence about their greasy cardigans and sweaty felt hats. The faces were normal, sunburnt, beer-anxious faces.

"Can you see, Danny Jordan?" asked the Comrade.

"Yes, Mr Mantle," I concurred, still not knowing what there was to see.

"Good! Get an eyeful! See all you want! Say a word about it and I'll kill you with my own hands."

"Yes, Mr Mantle." My stomach lurched with fear of the Comrade, who had a talent for successfully terrorising me. The street hummed and darkened, blurred and came clear again. Terror had passed like a bubble through my veins. If I had known the depths of the fears in which he threshed and which caused him to plague me, I would have spat at him and run home. But I could not tell then the relative importance of adults, all of whom were kings of the earth.

"Now look!" the Comrade murmured.

From the laneway beside the pub, home of SP bookie places, sly grog shops and worse, six men hurried towards the trucks.

54

"They're different men," Joseph breathed.

"That's right," the Comrade laughed. "They're *our* men!"

They were not so very different from the six who had recently gone into the public bar, not different at all to the casual eyes of the footpath drinker. Six weathered men had entered the bar, six weathered men slipped from the lane, split into three groups of two, lifted the bonnets in unison, reaching into the bowels of the motors, causing them to growl awake simultaneously. The crews climbed up to their cabins with an air of leisured possession, let their trucks howl for a few seconds at the kerbside, then swung them out evenly and rolled them past us. As they went by, the Comrade held his face away from them, but the men in the cabins were looking to the right, at all costs to avoid an accident a hundred yards from the pub. They turned into Deakin Street, *our* street, yelped into second gear along the railway embankment. Their noise vanished quickly, as if it had been stolen out of the air.

The Comrade stared at us, bright-eyed and triumphant.

"What's in the trucks?" Lennie whispered.

"Something precious, never mind. But it's ours now. My oath it's ours. One day when you're a grown man, Lennie, and everything's ours, you can think back to this Friday afternoon. You've seen the beginning of something very big.

"So've you two!" he added to Joseph and me; *but by the time what I say is consummated,* he implied, *Joseph will have been gathered in to his defective forefathers, and you, Jordan, will have cracked open with the gangrene of dogma.* "You can see how we get our way in this world."

Lennie hugged his father's thighs and looked straight

up along the line of the Comrade's shirt buttons, across the stubbled chin, around the pits of nostrils to the rims of his father's eyes.

"Comrade," he begged, "tell me what was in the trucks. Go on, Comrade. I'd never tell anyone. I'll spit and hope to die."

"Go on, Comrade!" Joseph chorused, far grimmer in matters of secrets than Lennie because he had only a few years into which to cram the mysteries and whispered things of life.

"When I'm feeling better I might tell you about it, son." The Comrade spoke softly and compassion curled up the corners of his mouth. "Now run off home and tell your mother . . ."

"But you . . .!" Lennie began to explain.

"You've already been shown more than you should." He shook his head wildly like a man who's walked into a tarantula web strung between trees. "I've got a pain in my head. Can't you get home when I tell you? Can't you, Lennie?"

He took one savage step towards the boy. His sons turned and loped away. I followed them, a little to their rear, to show that I was not bound by the same strong obedience. Their slumped little faces blinked to the afternoon sun as they turned into Deakin Street. The Comrade must have seen their humped shoulders through the rhododendrons, for he called across to them gently, "Tell Hilda I won't be long!"

An hour later, I was still paddling in the warm lees of daylight at the western end of our veranda, which was bridge and conning tower and centre of command. The Comrade came along. Inebriates fared badly in our street, since it sloped treacherously. Unable to curb their own momentum, they would take longer, wider steps until, opposite the viaduct, they were either trotting or prostrate. There was no doubt today. The Comrade had finished the job and was now quite nastily drunk.

I stiffened against the wall, breathless with chameleon desire. Even the best of drunks I hated, and hell was for me a place full of them. The Comrade's face was the face of drunkenness. There were no sober states for it; it was always at least passively drunk; it was daily more ugly, sad, gorged and incontinent.

He reined himself in at the gate. "Daniel Jordan!" he called, wavering above the gatepost like a beserk ectoplasm. I didn't move.

"Daniel Jordan, come over here you little bastard when I call you and don't stop there frigging about in the shadows!"

There was something compelling in what I then thought were the ultimates in obscenity. I approached him, thinking of the wrought iron gate between us.

The Comrade leant on the gatepost. "D'you know what was in those trucks?" he asked.

"No!"

"You're sure?"

"Yes!"

"D'you want to know?"

I didn't venture to say.

"D'you want to know?"

"All right."

"Then I'll tell you!" He leant across the gate and his breath stung my eyes like the effluvia of Old Finnie's secret beer vats.

"Arms and ammunition!" he hissed. *"Guns* and ammunition from the works up the line. Do you know what ammunition is?"

"Bullets?"

"Yes! Bullets! And there's one for you if you ever tell anyone. One of those in one of the trucks today'll go screaming into your little guts if ever you tell anyone. I'll *blast* it into you. The blood will pour out of you and you'll scream to your mother of course, but it won't be any use. She won't be able to get that bullet out."

I shuddered for love of the frenzied mother I could see kneeling over a small son retching up blood.

"As long as you understand," the Comrade said. The words fluttered on his lips together with the constant, small and flatulent noises of a stomach drunk on ale.

I stood crying softly for a while and was shocked to see him gone when I looked up again. The street was empty; no homey train thundered down from Parramatta; the wires above the lines swayed in a dusk westerly. The world was incommunicative on purpose now. It wanted me to go inside; and in view of the travail before her, to treat my mother as a first lady.

9

There was a period of cosmic holiday when the Comrade vanished for a fortnight. Neither early with gory hand, nor on time and pontifical, nor late and screaming drunk did he come back to his people. Apart from his body not having appeared in the morgue nor rolled up goose-fleshed and nibbled from the Harbour's slime, Hilda had no comfort. In the meantime, gossip at the corner, small talk over the counter were murderous hazards for her pride. The deadly neutral question, "How's your husband these days?" (*and where the hell is he?*) sliced her soul open like a saveloy.

She was not a good liar. She could not fabricate an iron-bound strand of lies and drag her dignity above the level of the waters. And, even so, her eyes were eternally raw from cupboard crying.

Like the priests of a departed god who honoured their grove no longer, the boys lingered by their peach tree, dazed and obscurely guilty. Their games now were the scanning of train windows for his face, the watching of corners for him to turn them. Hilda had assured them. He would definitely be back.

One afternoon he came down from the station like the

best of the bourgeoisie, and hurried down Deakin Street. In the instant Lennie's rapt face squealed, Joseph also sighted him. They ran off, each in his varying style; and the Comrade jolted to a stop as he saw them coming to claim him. He was very pale, I noted as the three came closer. He carried his coat over his elbow and there was a sagging lump in one of his pants pockets. It wasn't as I thought, a bag of gobstoppers. It was the several parts of a Mills hand-grenade.

And don't, Aunt Verna counselled by letter from Mackay, *go loaning money earned by Brian on the field of battle to make up for money not earned by a radical tramp at the abattoirs.*

When the Comrade had first disappeared a few Fridays before, it had been characteristically, with his pay. Hilda had then taken out a third of her savings, and spent three pounds on having Joseph tested by the Macquarie Street specialist who convinced her the boy was incurable, but promised that if any likely cure were found, he would write and tell her. On the other two, the Mantles lived for ten days. Finally, Hilda approached my mother. She had no right, she admitted, to ask for a loan of money, but she had to keep a tenner in the bank for Joseph's sake. *If a cure were found for Joseph, Stell, and there was no money to pay for it, well,* that would be the ultimate irony. "How much do you want, Hilda?" asked Stell.

But her eyes hooded with anger when Hilda visited us on the morning after the Comrade's return with two bottles of lemonade and, of course, the boys. She *was* in debt to us, Hilda began. *Indeed,* replied Stell. The word flopped onto the lineolum like a dead fish. But now that the Comrade was repentantly back at work (piece work only, which was all the management would give him any

60

more; wouldn't have got that without the union); now that he had woken up to himself, Hilda was assured of wages at the end of the week when our money would be repaid. Surely no one would begrudge her her little celebration. No one did. We got down five glasses and a plate of drab and circumspect war effort biscuits.

There was only one way to drink aerated waters, and that was as swiftly as, at the far end of the scale of delight, Socrates had drunk the hemlock. The aerated part of the whole thing set off delicious rumblings, starting in the pit of the stomach, thundering up the throat. It was Lennie who gave incipient signs of the Etna in his small, tough bowels. Wherefore we were all sent outside to be pigs beneath an open sky.

"So much for the Sons of Thunder," said my mother.

There was heavy grass along the galvanised fence where for half an hour we played *Scorched Earth*. Until Lennie called us over to view a green beetle on a paspalum stalk. It looked harmless, he conceded, but it had hidden claws and a sac of poison which could burn through steel. The Comrade had seen an Aborigine stung by one of these beetles, and the poor black's veins had knotted and blown up like balloons, until they split and blood gushed out of his ears like water from a burst main. With his limited grasp of words, Lennie dispatched his problematical abo with a fever of pink buboes. Our minds licking around the image of Lennie's fantastic tick, we ambled up to the laundry's blue shadow, reclined on the cement and listened for the venom which might in the next instant dement our hearts and dry our blood to a crust. After a wait of fifteen minutes, there was no palpitation, no scabrous splotch. It was apparent; we would live.

We stirred our limbs, eyed the sun which moved in a slow arc over the highway. But we did not step out to face it. For, unaccountably, there was an alien voice raised high in the kitchen.

I stalked to the wire-gauze door, Gunga Din in the Nabob's camp. With no other noise than air whistling through Joseph's imperfect nose, the Mantle boys crowded beside me, laying their flanks down inch by inch on the concrete step. In turn, we raised an eye above the level of the gauze, glimpsed the cavernous room still warm with the smell of breakfast porridge, surveyed it for a half-blind instant, then snatched our heads down again to the level of the steps.

Inside was some strange woman. Before her strangeness, Hilda and my mother had retreated until they were backed against the dresser with its Coronation of George VI milk jug. The stranger differed astoundingly from them.

She had wide lips which quivered with a sodden sort of comment on such things as the Coronation milk jug. Her crooked mouth changed form as often, as irregularly as an amoeba. Her hair fell blonde and stringy, motleyed with dirt or diluted peroxide, on to shoulders motleyed with dirt or sun spots. Her orange crêpe dress began behind her neck, ignored her shoulders, widened down her front in time to clothe her breasts, and cascaded drably from her thighs. The curves of her body sagged fulsomely over her perpendicular lines, flaccid mangoes sagging from the tree. Her legs were bare and she wore open-work shoes. It was a summer dress for a pierside heyday; and she must have been cold when she came up against the northerly blowing that day. Not that she lacked climatic sense nor even a sense of clothes. It suited her to be tinsel before Hilda.

"I'm not saying, luv," she claimed, "that he's not finished with me. My bloody oath he's finished! I wouldn't let him in the house again. All I'm saying is I

kept that gentleman husband of yours for two whole —
let's call them damned, luv, there's ladies present — two
whole damned weeks. I fed him. I lent him money to
gamble with and he went bloody mad at the baccarat
last Friday night. I don't know why I financed him.
There's a sort of poxy charm about him at first. I s'pose
that's what got *you* in. Luv!''

She daubed the word *luv* across Hilda's cheeks like
slime. I could hear the orange crêpe swish as the lady
swung her hips controversially; I could hear Hilda,
wifely, plump, tight with rage, grunt at the cruel loose-
limbed vulgarity who had barged into her little festival.

"I don't want you in here," Hilda murmured. Her
furry voice came queerly to us, as quiet as the eye of a
cyclone sucking in its breath for the purposes of
mayhem. "This is my friend's home. How in the name
of Holy Suffering Mike you knew I was here I don't
know!''

"A neighbour was passing by when I knocked at your
place," the orange crêpe lady interposed chattily, "and
she said I could try here. Lucky I did, luv. I mightn't
never have found you.''

"I don't care how you got *here*. I don't want you in
my place. And if you don't go now, I'm going straight
to the corner and ring for the police.''

The woman laughed. There was no dole in the laugh,
but it told us that this lady had found out that the police
were a weak and erratic recourse, and that she herself
had been unwelcome in innumerable people's kitchens
for years. To be unwelcome in Hilda's and ours was for
her no new frontier.

"I don't think you would, luv," she said. "You're
too damned proud. I can tell it. You're fat with bloody
pride. And you wouldn't want a couple of constables
tramping round in here sneering at the lot of us. And

63

you know, luv, they would sneer. Particularly at you. I mean to say, your husband owes me for more than just food and board and the loan of a few quid. The police'd know all this. They'd say, 'Well, the one in the orange might be a fancy lady but that's the last thing the other one is, as far as her husband's concerned. That's the last thing she is, *fancy*.' "

Still hunched by the gauze door, we could hear Hilda choking, conjuring up a blow or a word to keep the Comrade's absence simply a dull and faceless loneliness, not a keen, well-detailed shame involving the woman in orange crêpe. Lying on the step, sweating on the side of me which was half-buried in Lennie, and cold on the side pressed hard into the pores of the cement, I could sense that for some reason the orange crêpe lady was unanswerable.

But before Hilda could spit out a word, it was my mother who spoke up, quite baritone and furious.

"Hilda, get this woman out of my house. She isn't my disgrace. I won't have her in here. I won't have myself and Daniel getting involved in your shame. I won't have a harlot discussing what your husband owes her in my kitchen!"

"Stell," Hilda protested softly, "it isn't my fault, Stell!"

"Of course it's your fault! Have you ever thought of leaving him?"

"And you're supposed to be a Catholic!"

"Oh, Hilda! Don't tell me you love him. This whore and God knows how many others and God knows how many in the future . . . he loves them all better than he loves you."

"Don't say that, Stell! Don't say that sort of thing if you want to keep a friend. It's drink that sends Len astray."

"Huh!" said the fancy lady. "He sends drink astray. He's sent a hell of a lot of it astray in the last fortnight."

"Look at the truth, Hilda! Your marriage is no good. You married the original no-hoper. Get out of it, leave him. If people point at you in the street as a woman whose marriage failed, then let them go to the other place!"

"He's a good weak man," Hilda claimed frantically. "You should see that. Surely Brian's got his weaknesses."

"Dear God, if Brian had the Comrade's vices he wouldn't be a good, weak man. He'd be an evil one, just the same as the Comrade is. I wouldn't be in the same room as the Comrade for two minutes. I don't think I've met a *more* evil man."

The boys turned pallid faces on me. Blasphemy had left them the bilious tint of young dripping. And yet they did not accuse me, their faces did not purple with rage. The three of us together embarked on a vague hatred of the fancy lady.

"Look, luv," the lady began again in the wake of my mother's spoken outrage, "I don't want to be persistent but he owes me about twelve quid. I'm willing to come to a settlement." (Here I rose on my haunches to review the room and saw the woman's mouth set in a long crooked grin, the lower lip on one side of her face having fallen away to show a bunch of nicotined teeth. Her shoulders shook satirically.) "I mean, I don't think you'd want an itemised account."

While the boys snatched a look each, their mother cursed the lady and wished her to be pickled in the depths of hell. We heard the lady slap some fleshy part of her body and laugh in metallic good humour.

"Get her *out*, Hilda!"

"But part of the twelve quid," the fancy lady went on

as evenly as a politician, "belongs to a friend of mine he borrowed it from. And with *that* money he bought something from a soldier."

"I've got nothing to lose, Hilda! I'll soon call the police."

"Oh, shut up, luv!" the fancy lady groaned. "This is important. The night before last a soldier came up to my place and gave something to beloved Len. I don't know what it was. It was all done up in a greasy cloth and when I wanted to see it, he yelled at me. 'Don't touch that,' he said. 'It's dangerous.' It could've been a gun or something. I mean, I'm not being nasty now, luv, and I've got no money reason like to tell you this. But he could be going to kill you or something."

The fancy lady was right. For the first time that morning she was not being nasty. We did not therefore anticipate her shriek, or the wide thud of her large unchecked body clopping to the floor. Violence dissolved all necessity for hiding. We tumbled into the kitchen.

The lady was on the floor, her dress up above her knees, one hairless lower leg doubled under her. The right hand corner of her brow was a mash of bruise and blood, her right eye-pit a well of gore as if the eye had been plucked out. My mother knelt listening for the fancy lady's tainted heart and Hilda staggered to a kitchen chair with a bloodied lemonade bottle in her hand, clutched by the neck.

Joseph proud-stepped up to her.

"The Comrade wouldn't kill you," he murmured, waited, thought all over his brow, and repeated, "The Comrade wouldn't kill you!"

My mother knelt upright, and glared at Hilda.

"Your husband's lady-friend's alive, Hilda," she announced. "What in the name of heaven are you going to do with her?"

"I don't know," Hilda said reverently, putting down the bottle.

"She'll need stitches."

"Yes, Stell."

Stell rose up. "I don't know how I'll ever forgive you, Hildie."

Hilda said nothing, running her fingers under the rim of her chair, looking at them for signs of dust.

"Look," my mother continued, "We'll put an overcoat on this blasted floozie, and we'll take her around to Dr Slattery."

"You'll have to wake her up."

"I'll wake the strumpet up."

Amongst the soft soap, kerosene, mouse-traps, scouring agents beneath the sink, Stell rummaged for the bottle of ammonia. She dragged the lady's blood-sticky head upright and pushed the opened bottle beneath her nose. The fumes needled at the lady's brain, jolting her head aside as neatly as any flush blow from men-friends of the Comrade's breed. Her shattered eyebrow they sponged with a strong solution of iodine, and when she squealed and rolled her head around, my mother clutched her by the back whisk of strawy hair, fixed the bleeding forehead in space and drenched it in a piercing wash of iodine.

The lady spat out a crisp awesome word I had heard only from a few fishermen at the Cape where old Finnie lived.

"Go and get your overcoat, Hilda."

Hilda swallowed a sad regurgitating crumb of violence.

"I'm sorry, Stell. I didn't know. I'm sorry. I'm terribly sorry."

"I'm not worried about that now. Get your overcoat. I'm not taking her half-naked to Dr Slattery. And I don't want *my* overcoat rotten with disease. You clouted her, Hilda. Now you clothe her!''

Lennie hugged Hilda, his arm going hardly more than half-way around her buttocks.

"Stay here with Mrs Jordan!" Hilda said to the boys.

The fancy lady shook her head, spilling dribbles of blood down her cheek.

"Hurry Hilda!" Stell called. "She's bleeding like a sow. And why not?''

"My overcoat, Stell?''

"Yes. And listen! We'll be all right. Dr Slattery won't find out anything from me. I promise you. And he won't believe this baggage against the word of two of his patients. So calm yourself down, Hilda. And *hurry!*''

"You'll pay, you lousy bitch!" the lady yelled vaguely as Hilda rushed out to find her overcoat. My mother administered again the iodine cure.

"You boys,'' she said, "go into the yard. Joseph and Lennie, don't take any notice of this rotten woman. Do you understand?''

"Yes, Mrs Jordan.''

"And when you go into the yard, stay there, *please!*'' The *please* was a quiet but not a soft one. It followed us towards the door like an Arctic, lean and subtle beast. Its ferocity was largely for the fancy lady, but it could not promise that if we vexed it it would not turn on us. The few paternal blasts of temper which had withered me in the past were cosy human weaknesses beside the tigress exasperation in Stell's voice. We walked backwards to the door, and the last thing we saw was Stell picking up a piece of medicated wadding she'd been saving, preparing to lay it like the upper half of a sandwich on the orange crêpe lady's eye, but waiting a second and laying it down considerably more gently.

*   *   *

"Your mother said a lot of *evil* things about the Comrade," Joseph commented. You could see that he didn't want to fight over the matter, being so profoundly hurt.

"But the *tart* said a lot of things that were worser." Lennie accepted insult more vigorously than his brother.

It was best to make conversation. "Aunt Verna got really mad at me for calling someone a tart," I said.

We were sitting in a peace-pipe circle on the lawn towards one o'clock. We had heard the ladies leave for Dr Slattery's ten minutes before, but the boys hadn't said much yet, being dazed. The earth was cold after the frost, but the sun was pleasant on Lennie's and my faces and on Joseph's shoulders. A fat magpie had flurried down and gone questing along the galvanised fence, waddling enough to entertain the Mantles for minutes on end.

"Anyhow, what's a tart?" Joseph asked. "I bet you don't know, Jordan!"

"It's a cake!" I was as prim as Aunt Verna could have wished.

"Don't try to be funny with me, Jordan," he murmured with a tragic sort of anxiety that I might. "It's a loose woman. That's what my grandmother told me."

"Loose woman?"

"That one was loose, all right?" Lennie giggled with enlightenment. "She had a backside on her like a couple of sugarbags and she wriggled it all over the kitchen."

We laughed a snide guilty laugh. I glanced a little respectfully at Lennie. No, he wasn't as clever as that. He must have heard that type of talk from the Comrade.

"And she said," Joseph spat at the memory, "that the Comrade was going to kill someone."

"He said he'd kill me!" I told them humourlessly, remembering the afternoon the ammunition trucks had been stolen.

69

"You know he didn't mean it, Jordan. Grown-ups are always telling kids they'll kill them. My grandfather told us that when we scraped the putty out of the windows at his place. And he wouldn't hurt an ant."

"The Comrade meant it when he said it," I insisted, "and anyhow, why's he bought a gun?"

Joseph ran his fingers over the lawn, picked a plum-pudding, a little sweet green plant that grew melon-shaped amongst the grass. He chewed it in a state of doubt.

"It wasn't a gun, Jordan. That's another lie."

"What was it then?"

Joseph thought. He had found another plum-pudding, and meditated until it was eaten.

"If you come next door," he said, "if you're game enough to come next door, I'll show you."

The fat magpie bustled into the air, aghast at this suggestion.

"You heard my mother," I said simply.

"All right then," Joseph murmured. "Then if you're too much of a dingo to come and see, then shut up."

"I'm not a dingo."

The plum-pudding habit spread. We sought them nervously in the grass and nibbled them down.

"What is it then?" I asked.

"You'll have to come and see, Jordan! Except that you're not game to do that."

Very pale, I shrugged.

"All right! Will it take long?"

"No!"

"All right! I'll go."

In the Mantles' kitchen the old table waited for us dimly. The lounge room was darker still. Slumped by one of the walls, with one leg raised stupidly from the uneven floor, was a long dark-varnished cabinet. Joseph flipped open its doors. Inside were a few dimity tablecloths, some glassware and, standing in the centre of the top shelf, upright and substantial like a party of aldermen, five hefty books.

"*Das Kap-it-al*," I read. "*The Spe-eches of — of Lenin*. Is that Comrade Lenin?"

"Yes," said Lennie securely.

"It isn't, stupid," Joseph grunted. "It's another Lenin."

"Is this all?" I asked, nodding towards the cabinet.

"No!" said Joseph. "I just thought I'd show you those books. Not many people've seen them."

"Well, hurry up! They might be back from the doctor's soon."

The north wind scuttled down their laneway, mouthing, "Hurry! Hurry!" Joseph turned to another cabinet, the child of the first, clogged with the same dark varnish, much squatter. He grasped its small white knob and rattled it to show that the cabinet was locked. It was from there on a matter of legerdemain for Joseph. He pulled a penknife from his pocket, gestured it in the air, drew out the blade and opened the door with it. Lennie and I knelt to look inside. But there was yet more to perform. Joseph guarded the entrance with an extended arm.

"Lennie," he said grandly, "did the Comrade send us all into the kitchen for a while last night?"

"Yes," Lennie gurgled. "He said he wanted us right out of here and don't dare come in till he told us we could."

"That's right. But *I* didn't stay in the kitchen."

"You went to the lavatory!" Lennie supplied.

"That's right, only I didn't. I came down the lane and looked in at this window. And that's how I saw what the

Comrade was putting in a box. Then he put the box in *this* cabinet."

"What was in it?" I shrilled.

"Look!" uttered Joseph. And he pulled out a box marked "Greene's Casuals for Particular Men" and half-full of packing straw. Even Lennie had seen enough Hollywood to tell what it was that sat up on top of the straw like a complacent Easter egg.

"It's a hand-grenade!" he yelled.

"Yes!"

A green melon with squares cut in its surface lay in the middle of the box. Surrounding it were a few shiny metal rods (one of them with a spring), a lever, a little wick-like fuse, a plug for the bottom of the grenade, and the pin which Clark Gable usually pulled out with his teeth.

"Let me see!" said Lennie, reaching for the grenade. Joseph slapped his hand.

"Get away! This is the Comrade's. I don't know what he wants it for, but he's probably working for the Army or the government or something."

In the dark room, from the deeps of the cabinet, from the grease caked on the grenade, I could smell death. It was necessary to stand up and back away from the shoebox.

"You aren't going to tell, Jordan, are you?"

"No," I said, confused, tipping backwards into an easy chair and thinking that it was the grave till its spongy seat sat me up straight in drab spaciousness.

"If it ever got out about this grenade, I'd let the Comrade know it was you who blabbed. You're my friend, but the Comrade's my father."

I wriggled up out of the puffy arms of the easy chair. It occurred to me that there was no need to maintain a friendship involving terror of the Comrade, secrets of deathly things (ammunition trucks and grenades), and the intrusion of the orange crêpe lady.

"Who said I want to be your bloody friend?" I roared at them. They raised their pallid faces to me. The Mantles were notable for their pallor, and when one challenged their fundamental tenets, such as that it is an ultimate honour to be known by the Comrade, they whitened prodigiously.

"Who said I want to be your bloody friend?" I repeated, since it had startled them the first time.

Then I crossed the short darkness to the kitchen door, sped along the lane and within seconds was home again, breathing hard, utterly freed of the Mantles.

Still, at the table at night, in bed, I would hold my breath waiting for the green pod of amatol to blow the roof off the Mantles' place and shock all sense and order out of ours. But the house stood, and after a while I remembered the grenade only when a hearse pulled down the highway or Eucheria led us to pray for the departed.

73

10

Sister Eucheria looked out on her class. In their souls were crooked ways to be made straight, hills to be made plain, ruts of evil to be levelled. In Dolph Conlon's soul anyway, in each soul there, but not, I feared, in mine. Sister Eucheria feared this also.

I was a year younger than the others in the class which she was getting ready for First Confession. She would call me to the front of the class while the others were roaring their spellings, and as every mouth champed away at the letters and every eye consumed us, she would ask me about the faith, try to assure herself that I was at the age of reason, that there was some atom of absolvable guilt in me. For Eucheria was a humanist as well as a theologian, and feared to hurt me by omission from the Penance class as much as she feared to frustrate the Sacrament by presenting to it an innocent.

On a hushed, overcast Thursday morning, Eucheria lined us up in a corridor. A tall girl called Gwen Callan, who wrote the points up on the board for the Greens, who knew the four times tables as if they were the names of her own family, who had led the flower-strewers at Corpus Christi, who was without a doubt ripe for the purifying effects of the confessional, and who was in innumerable other ways perfect, strode in queenly fashion down the ranks straightening them, pulling poor Dolph into place by the snot-streaked sleeve of his blazer. The drill of the Sacrament was harboured in our minds; the words of petition, contrition, purpose of amendment marched up and down like brass bands. We scarcely spoke, plodding in strange silence beneath low secretive clouds. Westerlies pushed leaves the size of venial sins around the presbytery backyard, below the presbyterial washing. We had nearly come to the porch when Dolph hissed at me, "Look," and turning my head, I saw the priest striding towards the sacristy between drying shirts, a small purple stole in his hand.

Someone tapped my fingers with Holy Water. We were in the nave, where the pews sat up possessively, prejudiced against children. There was an amber, wormwood smell about the dustiness of the place, about the dust which was the bones of martyrs washed to a powder by seas of time and grace.

"In here, Daniel Jordan!" Eucheria whispered. Her face shone, particularly at her coifed cheekbones. The empty church excited her, as if there were more of the Divine Presence for her to bask in by virtue of the emptiness. She knelt in a state of suppressed exultation. Dolph and I watched her and were astounded. There was in her a genuinely nuptial excitement.

Waiting for the priest, we trundled out varied Acts, Acts of faith, hope, contrition, love. Clause by clause, Eucheria gave us the words which we repeated to the pigeoned clerestories. The priest, who had fine black hair and was built heroically, his cassock binding a barrel-chested frame into the ways of the Lord, came down the aisle. He was not flushed with the glory of his work; he did not look into our faces as if we were all-

75

but-unspotted lambs, cropping the eternal hillsides; his gaze passed us by and focused on the darksome alcove of the baptismal font. Yet I was pleased with the workaday dignity of the man. After all, I knew that most of us could not by the most extreme figure of speech be called *lambs*; and there was an unfussed air of habit about the way the priest pulled shut his confessional door that showed that he knew it too.

". . . to love You above all things," Eucheria prayed, "even to the shedding of my blood."

We could hear the blunt noises of the large-framed priest settling into his seat.

". . . even to the shedding of my blood," we roared.

Dolph Conlon recited prayers with a strange fervid mannerism. He held up his head, eyes bright and fixed on the Kingdom. But at every blessed syllable — Eucheria recited prayers in the same way as poetry — he nodded his head profoundly. This peculiarity was laughable in some of the girls, who were merely out to convince Eucheria that they were lilies of Sharon. But Dolph *was* a saint, despite the ragged blazer with the mucous stains on its sleeves. If others had laughed at the way Dolph prayed, I would have tried to throttle them for it. But children are basically fair on these matters. They laughed at the lilies of Sharon, but not at Dolph.

For both Dolph and Sister Eucheria meant that "shedding of my blood" business. They would, for example, joyously have put their hands beneath a cleaver as Comrade Lenin had, although with them it would not have simply been a selfish craving for the euphoria of agonising for their cause which led them to it. But Dolph, Eucheria and the Comrade were a kindred to which we others did not belong. They were prodigal of blood, while there was nothing to which we were more firmly attached.

"Now you will examine your consciences," Eucheria announced, but I had raked mine over before falling to sleep the night before. We knelt in silence, and Dolph, with his nose pressed hard between joined hands, frowned as he lifted enormity after enormity from the black pits of his soul.

In fright, I shuddered upright. The nun was bending over me, smiling, trying to show that she would willingly go into the box with me but that that was not allowed.

"You go into that one, Daniel," she whispered.

A girl had already risen and swayed into the confessional as if she were Saints Perpetua and Felicity combined, flowing into the area. Important and terrified, first fruit of Eucheria's corner of the Vineyard, I went into what she called *the tribunal of mercy*, and jammed the ball-bearing door closed behind me. No one must hear my secret shame.

It was a little cell-like place with a high-up beaded window the colour of sago. There was a prie-dieu before the wire grille on which was tied a crucifix. Kneeling, I was just able to rest my nose on the bottom of the grille. During the confession then, I would have to stand, exposed head and shoulders to the terrible absolution of God. Beyond the grille, the sliding cedar shute was closed, but I could hear the girl on the other side of the priest's compartment telling him *fortissimo* that she had called her mother a fat old fool. When that happened, when you overheard another person's guilt, you didn't worry, Eucheria had said, you simply held your hands over your ears. Doing this, I strained forward to kiss Christ's pierced feet, and waited.

The cedar shute opened softly, and the priest held his head sideways to look down at me, for I still had my ears clamped and my eyes half-closed.

"Hello," he said, as if he were merely a baker or something similar.

"*Good morn-ing, Fath-er*," I recited euphorically.

"You're not worried, are you?" He spoke in the tone doctors adopted when they had the syringe in their hands. It was time for me to bring matters to order.

> "Bless me, Father,
> For I have sinned.
> This is my first
> Confession, Father!"

I announced in a flurry of dactyls and iambics.

"Yes," he said. "Now, you just *softly* tell me of the few little wrongs you've done. And don't be scared, because God is very pleased with you."

"There is a golden rule when you make a confession," Eucheria had told us. "*The worst first!*"

"I fight with Joseph Mantle, Father."

"I see. Well, I think all boys fight."

I would not have my viciousness minimised.

"But I start fights with him because I like to beat him."

"I see," he repeated, no way impressed.

"But Joseph Mantle's half a cripple," I announced climactically.

. "Oh! That's different. Are you going to do your best not to fight him in future then?"

"Yes, Father."

"Anything else?"

I sucked my breath in, formed my next heinousness on my tongue, and spat it out. "I hated a man!"

"Oh? Did you really hate him?"

"Yes!"

"Well, you've got to be really mad at a person to hate him, you know. You've got to wish he was dead and in

78

hell. I'm sure you didn't wish this about that man, did you?"

"Yes, Father!"

"You did." He seemed appropriately interested now. "Who *is* the man?"

"Comrade Lenin!"

"Who?"

"Comrade Lenin. He's Joseph Mantle's father. He's a colonist."

"A colonist? How do you mean?"

"He wears a red handkerchief with a hammer and — I've forgotten what else, Father."

"He wouldn't be a member of the Colonist Party?" the priest asked with quick insight.

"Yes!" I said.

"And is that the only reason you hate him?"

"No, Father. He punched me. He said he'd kill me."

The purple stole rose and fell as the priest shrugged. "First of all, are you going to forgive him?"

"Yes."

"Good boy. Now next, have you told your father about this Comrade fellow?"

"My father's in Egypt, Father."

"Well, have you told your mother?"

"No! I didn't tell her — he said he'd kill me."

"Well, he might have been joking anyhow. But tell her anyway. Will you do that?"

"Yes, Father!"

"Now make sure you tell her. Right?"

"Yes, Father!"

The priest half-stood up to stretch. Then he hid a yawn and began again.

"Now, I am going to ask you a very important question. I'm only asking you this so that we can stop this Comrade bloke if he's doing you harm. You tell me the truth, because I'm your friend. Now the question is, has the Comrade ever tried to do anything dirty and evil to you?''

"No, Father.'' I told him that the Comrade had threatened to shoot me if I ever told about the ammunition trucks.

"You see, my little friend,'' the priest went on, "if you tell your mother about all this, she can get the police to stop him if he tries to scare you again.''

"Yes, Father!''

"And tell your mother, if he ever troubles you, she can get help from me. My name is *Father Peters. Peters.* Will you remember that?''

"Yes, Father!''

"Yes. Just ask for Father Peters at the presbytery. Now, anything else?''

"Sometimes I hide in the long grass when my mother wants me to go and get the milk. And I tell lies.''

"All right! I think that will do you. Have you had a happy First Confession?''

"Yes, thank you Father. Oh, and Comrade Lenin cuts himself up with a meat cleaver. He goes out on constipation from the meat works and hands out newspapers for the . . .''

"For the Colonists?'' the priest asked intelligently.

"Yes!''

"You keep away from this Comrade Lenin fellow, won't you? And remember, Father Peters. As soon as he tries anything, come to me! Now, for your penance . . .''

I held the door open for Dolph, conscious for the first time of the notoriously long session I had had in the confessional. Three seatfuls of gaping uninitiates watched Dolph go in and me come out. Their large eyes washed me up and down, saying, "There goes a sinner

and a half." Then, on the strength of my new in-
nocence, I plodded up to the Lady Altar to speak with
the Virgin Mother.

The sun had rolled between two cloud-banks, and lit up
with a quick, invigorating fervour, the *St Paul-without-
the-Walls* facade of the church, and the line of children
standing below it. Intense was the gaiety of those thirty-
five infants as they waited for the priest and Sister
Eucheria to finish talking, in so far as the Seal of the
Confessional allowed, of the morning's work. Dolph
and I, at the back of the column, could hear fragments
of what was said.

"Definitely very young, Sister," the priest murmured. "I wouldn't recommend that they make their
Communion until towards the end of the year."

Sister Eucheria's reply was blown away as the wind
rose again and the cloud-banks moved in on our brief
sun.

"Well, to tell you the truth," the priest pursued,
"there were a few I couldn't absolve even with the most
conditional of absolutions. You can't absolve the utterly
innocent, you know Sister. There were a few of them I
simply blessed. That satisfied them. They thought
they'd been to Confession."

This statement of priestly policy I did not clearly
understand, and Dolph, with his native decency, did not
listen to. Yet I *did* understand that some of us had acted
in a tableau but no sacrament. I kicked at the pathway,
loosing an ankle-high spray of gravel. Here, as in other
fields, was the same daunting incompleteness that af-
flicted everything in which I was concerned. I had, for
example, won a card for being champion speller a few
weeks before, but champion speller of rows three and
four, the ungifted, unelect half of the class. I had been

given charge of children at the bubblers one day — but kindergarten children. People from my own class would have squirted me with supreme irreverence. And today, I could say I had confessed, but whether I had been to Confession or not, that only the priest knew.

Dolph, hazed with glory, and myself with a bone of disappointment lodged in my throat, gave no trouble to Eucheria as back we marched to class.

11

In June, talk of the Comrade's galloping degeneration followed us around like a condition of existence. We did not go out often, since the much pre-figured Herbie was to be born in July. Wherever we did go, people wanted to ask us about the Comrade and the way he was treating Hilda, about the eye-patch she'd been wearing which they were willing to bet covered no sty, about Lennie falling to sleep at school because of the yelling of abuse and hurling of cups and clothes-brushes which went with the Comrade's irregular homecomings. Where did he get all that drink from? the women on the corners wanted to know. They would have hated to see how bare *her* cupboard was, they all nodded.

It was true that, drunk, the Comrade was becoming a consistent wife-beater. Hilda would be thugged by him once, maybe twice, or even three times a week. She knew that we could hear the din of these beatings and, on the mornings after, would stagger into our place to tell us how contrite the Comrade was. And each time, my mother would give her tea and beg her to leave the brute but for heaven's sake, don't tell him she said so.

At the end of June, a week early, Stell gave birth to a

baby son. Aunt Pat, down from the Cape, took me up to the small maternity hospital, away from the soot of the railway and with young pines in its garden, and we visited the crowded little ward where the babies, with huge labels pinned on their gowns, lay three to a cot, indulging the shortages of a war of which they had little part. Some nurse with a decorative taste had put Herbie, black-polled and resolutely serene, in the middle of two bald girls who were bunching their minute fists and wailing with what was partly grief but mainly annoyance straight up into our faces. Pat laughed and said that they'd expected a cradle of their own and wouldn't have come had they known the accommodation was so lacking.

Through short, veering corridors we searched for my mother's room. The door of the labour ward was partly open and screams from inside sent us pale. A nurse came along, said "Those Italian women always panic!" and closed the door fully. She led us to my mother in a room dominated by snapdragons, roses and dahlias, rather than by the five quiet women lying there. Stell's cheeks and brow were white and half-transparent like polished soap. She had ribbons in her hair and seemed invincibly happy.

A day later, Herbie was named. Father Peters had come to the hospital to anoint a woman who had lost her child and was now dying herself. After the rites, he visited my mother to congratulate her.

"What are you going to call him,?" he asked her.

"I'd like to call him after my father," Stell said. "But that's impossible. He's an Irishman and his name's Finbar. People call him Old Finnie."

"But Finbar's just Irish for Brian," the priest told her. "My name's Brian and whenever I was called to Holy Orders, they'd announce me as Finbarrus Peters."

My mother quoted a Latin tag Old Finnie had taught her. "*Roma locuta* est, causa finita *est*," she said. "And my husband, who's in Egypt, his name is Brian, too."

One morning Pat, who was staying in Sydney for a while to be the baby's godmother, opened the door to get the milk and found her boyfriend, out of his God-abandoned training camp in the bush for the weekend, sitting on the back steps with his tunic collar up around his ears and dew on his hat. Although there seemed nothing delectable about Pat, her eyes swollen from sleep and her dress not yet properly settled on her loping country-girl body, her soldier beamed at her and managed to kiss her obliquely on the forehead before she told him to wake up Australia and come inside, he must be frozen to death.

"It's been a bit cold out there," he admitted. "My greatcoat's in at the railway." He thought it gallant to have a greatcoat. "Goodday, Dig!" he called to me where I sat spooning over an unmilked bowl of rolled oats. My mother was home and my new brother. It was Saturday and a Saturday I didn't want to share with a young soldier when soldiers were tuppence a dozen and one no longer accepted them on the basis of their uniform alone. As well, he had caught me with my pyjama top on. It was an unheroic beginning! I elected not to cultivate this nineteen-year-old man who stood across the table rubbing his hands and saying, "You wouldn't have another bowl of that, Pat?"

"This is Noel," Pat told me. "You remember Noel. He's from the Cape. He knew you when you were a baby. Say *hello, Noel!*"

"Hello, Noel!" I said challengingly, implying that he'd find it insufficient *now* simply to tickle me under the chin, implying that anyhow I didn't give a damn about the pyjama coat. When my mother appeared and made him welcome, I could foresee a spoilt Saturday with Pat's soldier around the place washing his socks and getting Pat to sew on his buttons. It was too late to sit up and look receptive of an invitation when Noel unexpectedly offered her a morning in the shops, lunch somewhere, and after that the pictures or the races or fabled Luna Park or the Zoo. They rollicked off to the station together before nine. From next door, the Mantle boys saw them and waved them on their way, being born wavers, having waved the comings and goings of the Comrade since before they could walk.

They hadn't gone long, Pat and her trooper, when the door bell rang. We approached it trying to guess whose silhouette it was on the other side of the wrinkled glass, wanting to be sure it wasn't the Comrade's before we opened it. When my mother did, it was Mr Conlon, Dolph's father, a wiry little man with large hoary eyebrows and straight grey hair. He had a box of vegetables on his shoulder.

"Mrs Jordan," he said softly, lifting the brim of his Akubra with one knotty finger. "I met you and your husband at the football once. I'm Greg Conlon. The wife sent me down with some vegetables for you."

Invited in, he stood in the hall, a very unassertive little man. I had always thought of him as a large, square man, for he was a famed anti-Communist organiser at the abattoirs, and often Sister Eucheria asked the class to pray for him in his dangerous task.

"Come right through, Mr Conlon," my mother said, "and have a cup of tea."

Mr Conlon lumped his box down on a kitchen chair and began to empty it.

"There's a few pounds of peas," he mumbled, "and potatoes have been a ridiculous price. And I hope you like the peach conserve. Jean — that's the wife — makes enough of it each summer to drown in.''

"How can I thank you?''

"Better if you didn't. Excuse me.''

He walked across the room and pulled aside the curtains with green hillsides and bunches of bananas on them. His nose close up to the glass, he smiled. "Old Comrade Mantle. Your husband told me he lived beside you.''

I looked but was not tall enough to see past the Mantle's side wall and lavatory at the same slant angle at which Mr Conlon eyed the Comrade leaning against his far fence in the morning sun.

"Do you know him?'' my mother asked.

"I'll say I do, Mrs Jordan. I never met a dirtier moron. He's getting to be an embarrassment to the other Reds even.''

"How's that?''

"Well, if he keeps skipping work much longer, they'll just have to let the management sack him. Which'd mean they'd lose a very handy *robot*. That's a fellow who does exactly what he's told. I suppose you know, Mrs Jordan, that he often slices himself up with a cleaver to get time off for Party work.''

Mrs Jordan told him that we did certainly know this.

"Apart from that too many of the true Reds detest him. It's hard even for them to admire such a monumental bludger. I mean, if they're pretending to be the Party of the workers, the upholders of the rights of the proletariat, well, they can't very well use blokes like that as the symbol of the Party.''

Mr Conlon stayed at the window, grinning at the unaware Comrade.

"He's given me a lot of worry,'' my mother said, and

she and Mr Conlon swapped a glance which told that he knew exactly what she meant and that I didn't.

"Besides that, he has a bad effect on Daniel. He seems to disturb him."

"That'd be just about up to his weight," Mr Conlon nodded. "Well, let's not waste the morning on that brand of vermin." And he pulled the banana curtains together.

Having viewed the baby and played with its incredible little hands, Mr Conlon declared he'd have to go; he had to take the boys for a haircut. I thought warmly of my friend Dolph having his angular head barbered, and helped my mother convoy Mr Conlon to the door. There we discovered that he was yet another of those Irishmen who talk best on a doorstep when, threatened with the likelihood of departure, they have not so definitely departed that they cannot spare you an extra ten or so thousand words.

He was propped sideways to the door, speaking of the war, the Labor Party, the Communist Party, the Church, education, when the Comrade issued from the Mantle place, bound for the paper shop or for that sly grog lane beside the Glasgow Arms. Whatever it was that turned the Comrade slowly out of his gate and brought him ambling by our place, it was an eventuality which both he and Mr Conlon would mourn for the rest of their lives.

"I've spoken to a heck of a lot of American soldiers," Mr Conlon was saying at the time, "and they say that MacArthur has so many enemies in the Democratic Party, that he's being starved of men and supplies."

"Thank God he was supplied with enough to save us!" my mother responded with nervous piety. But she gave up all show of normal conversation when the Comrade halted before the gate and leant his folded arms along the gate-post. For a while he eyed us, one eyebrow down, one up, an aspect of him which recalled the smile of the orange crêpe lady. He grinned in his languid, boozy way. By then, Mr Conlon had become conscious of him.

"Well," murmured Mr Conlon, "some people are lucky!" Irony, however trite, became the hour. "Mornin', Comrade!" he called lustily.

"Dear Mrs Jordan!" The Comrade wagged his head in burlesque civility. "You've had a man in to fix the sewers. I seem to remember that man, Mrs Jordan. He was a shop steward once. A big unionist. A friend of the workers. He used to be a puppet of Archbishop Kelly. But he's changed now. Now he's a puppet of Archbishop Gilroy."

"None of that's too original," Mr Conlon whispered proudly. "The Reds have been saying that sort of thing about me for years."

He spoke up to the Comrade.

"Whose puppet are you, Mr Red? Report in to Mr Engels and get him to renew your strings! You look a wreck!"

"I have a hard life," the Comrade called back. "We all do. We all have to work too damned hard."

"Never mind, Saint Molotov. There's always heaven to look forward to."

"Fat consolation!" the Comrade grimaced.

Both men fell quiet while an old couple tottered past in their best, the lady with an extravagant collar of broad lace, and her small husband jiggling a watch chain across the most bourgeois of little bellies.

"Yes, a fat consolation!" the Comrade repeated when the old people had gone.

In return, Mr Conlon became whimsical. "I don't know, Comrade! An eternal meat-cleaver, an infinity of fingers to whack away at, an infinity of blood to bleed away with, an infinity of Compensation schemes to cover the whacking and the bleeding. I think you'd enjoy it, Len."

Our visitor smiled broadly, and my mother, led to it perhaps by mere politeness to a guest, made the same mistake. It came to the Comrade that he was being ridiculed. He straightened and pulled his arms to his sides. His face became blue. He spat.

"Are you laughing there, Mrs Jordan?"

My mother, in an instant, swallowed her smile.

"Are you laughing there?"

"Why not?" Mr Conlon yelled. "Why shouldn't she laugh? Perhaps you think she should be reverent. Or perhaps she should be afraid. Like the boy here." He designated me by clamping a bony hand down on my scalp. "Listen, Comrade! You're laughable! That's all! Laughable!"

But the Comrade's fury was not diverted. He stood immobile, totally absorbed in Stell's having smiled in ridicule of him.

"Would your husband laugh, Mrs Jordan, if I write to him and tell him that you're mucking around with our brave unionist?"

"He'd laugh all right! Do I look like a lady's man, Comrade?" Mr Conlon asked. His tongue rolled wryly within his cheeks. His wiry little body seemed on the verge of pouncing into the garden and thence at the Comrade's throat.

"I don't know what you look like, Conlon. You look like some sort of bloody fawning insect to me."

His grease-grey cardigan flying with passion and the morning breeze, the Comrade stepped back from the post. Seer-like, he stretched his right hand in front of him, and one damaged finger quivered at Mr Conlon on the veranda.

"I'll bring your house down around your damned ears, you clerical arse-licker."

"Go back home, Comrade! I've been threatened by experts. Go and have a blasted shave! You look as if you crawled out of a rusty tin."

A volley of sneezes shook the Comrade's dissolute shoulders in proof of Mr Conlon's insult. Three or four times he had to swallow before he could say, "I'm not threatening, you whore of bishops and monsignors. But when you go up in a great red blast, you just think that it was *me* who sent you. I want you to know that Len Mantle sent you hurtling into the Garden of Eden. And all the Garden of Eden is, Mr Shop Steward, is a bloody great brick wall the dead crash into. I'll hurl you at it so hard and fast you'll be in bits. The almighty union man'll be dead, and his great God won't stop him from turning into a stew of putrid muck."

He bit at the air, breathless from his pell-mell jeremiad.

"I'll send you all up!" he concluded, and his mind dressed the image of the grenade in coatings of lustre and secrecy and valour. An honest enough looking smile settled on his face, and we could barely hear him whisper, "So go to hell!" Remembering the morning paper and the sly grog or whatever it was, he jerked around and made his fugged way up Deakin Street. The faces on the veranda followed him.

"There goes a sweet one," said Mr Conlon.

Unnoticed, I put my head down on the doorjamb and closed my eyes. There was an instant's blackness, but in its centre a mote of yellow flame sprang up and spread, eating the dark away, opening up a blue abyss. I held my breath and waited to hit the Comrade's brick wall. But my mother's hand went around my neck and pulled my head up.

"See, Mr Conlon?" she murmured, cupping me by the ear against her hip. "See what I mean about Daniel and the Comrade?"

12

"Why do you want to know?" Uncle Matt asked me.

"I had an argument with a boy in my class." I paused on the lie, considered it, set it aside for Father Peters' absolution, another item amongst the assembled data which would prove to him that I was as maliciously evil as any other human.

"About grenades?"

"About how they work."

He rolled his eyes at the ceiling and whistled. "Kids these days!" he groaned.

It was the mid-afternoon of the same Saturday. We had entertained Pat's trooper for breakfast, Mr Conlon for morning tea, though he wouldn't have any, and now Matt had come, to lunch with his sister and see the new baby. Though it had squeaked at him irritably and once only, wrinkled the corners of its ancient little eyes, and slept again, Matt seemed well satisfied. As we talked, the baby was still sleeping, slung in his lambswool snuggery in the lounge room, his lilliputian hands either side of his chin, palms up, clenched, paw-like. My mother had gone for a walk in the sun to the chemist's.

I fetched the writing pad and a blunt pencil.

"There's this big green thing," I said, drawing an egg-shape, "and it's got these markings on it." I drew squares over the surface of the egg. It looked unjustifiably like a grenade when I'd finished. I was certain that I could draw the contents of the Comrade's shoebox with passable craftsmanship.

"That *big green thing*," Matt smiled, "is fat with amatol. It goes off like judgment day. Every one of those things cost the government ten quid."

"Why's it got marks like a pineapple on it?"

"To help it explode into fragments. You know, little bits. The government's got to get its ten quids' worth."

I sketched the pin.

"What does it do?" I asked.

He laughed in a superior way, as if I were simple enough to think that the egg and the pin were the total secret of a hand grenade. Without looking at him, I drew the shaft with its spring, the striker, the plug, the little fuse.

"Whoo there, Nana!" he grinned. "Where in the hell did you see all this?"

"I saw it — oh, a lot of places."

"Where, for example?"

"At the Easter Show they had one in a glass case."

He wrinkled his chin in comment on the wisdom of the people who ran the Easter Show.

"You've got a heck of a memory, Danny-boy!"

"How does it all work?"

The chair squealed as he leant back, wooing memory with his tongue in his cheek.

"Give me a look at what you've drawn, please. You'd better give me the pencil too."

For a long time he stared at my diagrams, until I began to believe that he knew nothing about grenades.

Once or twice he made a slow amendment to my work without any sign of confidence.

"That's more or less it," he mumbled at last. "Look here! This little fuse thing they call the detonator. And it's got a little metal cap on it, like this."

"How does it work?" I persisted humourlessly.

"Well professor, I know! Doesn't that amaze you, you bloody little smart alec?"

He slapped me across the shoulders then, and we wrestled for a while.

"But aren't you going to show me?"

"All right, damn it all."

With the pencil in his clenched fist, he demonstrated how the sprung shaft fitted down the centre of the grenade and was held by the lever which was held by the pin. He showed how the striker fitted into the base and how the detonator was inserted.

"Then all you do is screw in the plug."

If you pulled the pin, then threw the grenade, the lever fell free, the shaft plunged and hit the striker, which set off the detonator, which detonated the high explosive, which blew every bloody thing around to pieces, or so Uncle Matt said.

"From the time you pull that pin, Danny-boy, you've got four seconds."

"In the pictures they've got seven seconds."

"Yes, but they're bloody wonders, those Yanks. Why, if you had seven seconds, the Japs'd throw it right back at you. Then you'd be up — up a certain street."

I stared at the diagram which Matt had now laid down. There was a lack of most adult brands of concentration in him, and it had him instantly on his feet, sparring at the banana bunch curtains.

"If you look at the bottom of the grenade there are two holes, aren't there?" I asked.

"Yes." The curtains sighed beneath his volley of punches.

"And you put the top of the det — you know, the fuse thing, in the hole that doesn't go right through," I recited.

The jabbing fists stilled. He leaned back from the window and thought.

"You put the top of the detonator in the hole . . . that's right. Listen, you haven't found any of these grenade things, have you?"

"No!" A lie, once out, might as well be workmanlike. "No! There's a boy in my class thinks he knows everything!"

The fists remained frozen, the head statuesquely cocked.

"Well," I ventured, "he gave a talk on guns yesterday. You know, big guns. He had pictures and everything. I want to give a talk on grenades."

The concept of Eucheria admitting the roar of artillery into her pretty classroom was in itself such an unconscionable lie that I felt my eyes bulging with fright. If Matt forced me into the truth and stormed next door to pulp the Comrade for terrorising us with a piece of Her Majesty's most deadly equipment, it would make a sweet Saturday. But when Matt went back to camp, there would be pitch nights and wet Tuesdays and doldrum Wednesdays when the Comrade could have his way with us. *Mary, Mother of God, make him believe this lie which will be my last lie ever*. In the prayer were palpably involved far more layers of mind and appetite and animal apprehension than in the easy gabble of contrition I had recited to Father Peters. *If you make him believe this last untruth, I will love my neighbour the Comrade, I will convert Lennie, I will never again get new boys to wet from the far side of the boys' line.*

Matt nodded.

"D'you want to see your damned old uncle fight?" he asked.

"Where?"

"In a stadium, boy. Blast it all! In Leichhardt bloody Stadium. A four-round semi-final. Army versus Navy. The divisional champ gets sick. So who does the whole bloody Seventh Division want to fight for them? Why, that veteran of the Syrian campaign, the hero of Bardia, Sergeant Matthew Jordan."

I couldn't understand him but clapped lightly. He received the applause with a wide gesture of his hand.

"And I'm going to take *you*! I'll tell you, we'll get this youngster, what's his name? Noel! We'll get him with us and see you don't clear out with the prize money."

Quickly I reviewed the half-forgotten diagrams, tore them up and put the pieces in the waste box near the sink. Memorising what I had just destroyed, I walked back towards Matt. I could feel the memory of the Stadium slackening what I believed were most practical and vital fears. The mothering noise, the high-up secretive lights, the nervy wanness of fighters became in a few seconds keenly desirable as symptoms of a large manish sanity which would however, like Matt's protection, prevail only for an hour or two.

"Don't you want to come?"

"Yes!" I said. "How do you throw it?"

"Throw what?"

"A grenade."

"Oh hell!" he said.

13

I can remember the fight night as a sharp spell of joy. We cut importantly through queues with our free tickets. We loped through entrances which no one else could use. We waited in a yellow corridor beneath the bleachers while Matt consulted no one but the manager of the Army boxing troupe. We strolled into the bar where the belts of old champions, barnacled with metal work and imitation rubies, hung sterile of cut, contusion and brain bruise above the bottles.

Matt sat me on the counter and the barman whistled and said, "You're starting him on it young, Dig!" Noel had a beer. I had lemon squash. "I'm fighting," said Matt.

Noel and I took to our seats in the front about eight. A man in a bow tie, whom everybody whistled, climbed into the ring and welcomed the members of HM Forces. The proceeds of the night, he said, would go to the British Empire Fund. A sailor in the front called to the man in the bow tie to go and do something or other — I couldn't hear precisely — to the British Empire Fund. There were cheers and uproar. Thank you, said the man in the bow tie. Again, there were cheers and uproar. The first bout, the man persisted, was a bantam-weight quarter-final.

A small sailor crawled into the ring and faced a small airman. Around us, bets and flasks of spirits were passed with speed and a modicum of secrecy. The bell tolled tinnily, cheaply, joyously. The little men eyed each other for a short second, pounced in and began a breathless rough-house. In round four, the little airman simply fell over and didn't have the strength to get up.

To begin with there were four such fights, superb grudge fights; and the referee had to put forward all his strength, and military police had to hover up to the corners, before the fighters could be pulled apart at the end of each round. A spirit of delicious, just-legal mayhem pervaded the tiers of beery faces stretching up towards quarter-lit bleachers.

"The next bout is a semi-final of the middle-weight division," the man in the bow tie said at last. It would be over four rounds between Sergeant Matt Jordan and some sailor or other. Very soon, we knew that Matt was bound to lose. The sailor was intent within his large white stoker's body. Even beside Matt's Cape-bred olive trunk, he seemed savagely Italianate. And he clearly desired to win, a purpose not prominent in Matt's motives for becoming involved in the Service championships.

The sailor was a nimble man, nimbler than Matt, who stood by sponging in blow after blow without reeling. At the flurry of dance-steps and trim jabs which was his enemy, Matt gazed and concentrated for an opening, seeing one through the pain and sweat in his eyes and jolt of his head, and unleashing too late punches which would have felled a telegraph pole. In my mind frolicked the stubborn image of Matt sparring with the banana bunch curtains.

Towards the end of the first round, he lost his temper. He dropped his guard and seethed at the sailor, while the sailor had his way with Matt's eyes and ears, nose and jaw. When the round ended, the referee managed to persuade Matt to sit down.

"If he gets one of those hay-makers of his on that sailor's chin," Noel said, "it'll be goodnight, sailor!"

But defeat sat heavily on my stomach like a surfeit of something sticky.

To begin the second round, Matt hared out across the ring before the sailor had properly left his corner and was standing pushing at his mouth-guard with a gloved hand, and thwacked him across the jaws. The sailor tottered, the referee let the fight continue, the sailor's friends wished multiplex obscenities on Matt's head, and the troops roared, "Rip it into him, Dig!"

The sailor shook his head and Matt clouted him above the eye. In that second the bout became a brawl, for the sailor survived Matt's foray, but lost precision and self-control as well as a drop or two of blood. "He's opened the bastard's eye up," a soldier screamed. "You'll do us, Dig!" For three short uproarious minutes, the sailor and Matt hailed on each other a series of goliath clouts. One possessed, barbaric yell hung and shifted like a haze in the lighted space between dome and ring. The bell clanged dimly, making continued fighting an assault in law. The referee, trying to part the two, was clearly explaining that no one could win if both men ignored the bell. He waddled around them, pleading in one ear, then in the other. Moustachioed with blood, his back brilliantined with sweat, Matt's gothic figure had regressed from all human reasoning. Military police tried to mount the ring, but a cordon of sailors blocked them, roaring, "Give 'em a go!" The military police began to twirl their truncheons. We could all but hear the referee begging the sailor, mouthing each word for its long journey to the half-drowned mind. We could see the sailor's partly turned head, the cleft eyebrow seeping meatily down one side of his face. A few seconds before the military police threatened their way into the ring, the sailor stood back from Matt and crashed his fist into the referee's mouth. The referee reeled to the ropes and fell across them, while the people on that side of the ring whistled cruelly at his face crumpled with shock, and his lips mouthing blood.

Two provosts dragged Matt from the sailor, dressed him in his gown and escorted him along the aisle. He walked like a drunkard, his head was down, but we cheered him and wept with pride.

"That's my brother-in-law," Noel told the soldier next to him, a presumptuousness which in the éclat of that moment was easy to forgive.

"You'll do us, Dig!" the soldiers roared.

Later in the night, the loudspeaker called Private Noel Dalton to the Army dressing-room. We rose immediately, obviously initiates, obviously essential people. Speculative eyes followed us, but it was below us to glance back at them. We carried our mystery lightly away on our shoulders.

Matt lay on a table in the dressing-room, a medical orderly sitting beside him, sponging the viscid gore away from his nose. He just wanted, he said quietly, to make sure Noel would take me home. He had to go to hospital. They thought he had a broken nose. He seemed very sick.

We both told him what a tremendous fighter he was.

Sydney is a rainy city, I was to learn years later from a geography text. Twice as sunny as London, twice as rainy. Rain poured down with sub-tropical ardour, but not in any rainy season. Out of ash-grey thunderheads massing in from the beaches to the mountains after a day of sweat, out of ochre-fringed cumuli sitting up like judges where the winter sun went down, rain fell decisively if at all, with deliberate intent, its eye on the chance of washaway and flood and the dousing of best clothes.

It was such rain that woke me later in the night; certainly it was not Joseph with a coin in his fingers, tapping at the window. I turned on the pillow and saw him beyond the glass, staring like a runny oil portrait, his hair washed down into his eyes. "Let me in!" he mouthed as laboriously, as soundlessly as that piteous referee earlier in the night.

I stood upright, tottering on the new springy mattress, to feel behind the blind for the window catch. All our windows were locked now of a night. Though I couldn't see cause for it, I knew it had reference to the Comrade, to his always looking sly and speaking in a low voice to Stell whenever they met in the street. Even on the mildest of nights my mother locked up completely, grunting with anger when the catches were hard to force. And then, in secrecy, apart from the one time I had seen her do it, she would put a claw-hammer under her pillow.

Whenever it rained, the catches were stiff. I laboured with the window while Joseph's patient, frightened, soft-boiled eyes bleared up at me through the glass. When the catch gave, it gave with a rush. I swayed and the bed groaned like a bass violin. My shoulder pushed at the frame; the window went up with a series of short gasps. Joseph slithered into the room head-first, wheezing and in sodden pyjamas. He righted himself and waited shivering, dripping rain into a small, gleaming pool at his feet. His ankles were caught in the rectangle of moist light from the railway.

"It's cold," he grunted, smothering a sneeze in his pyjama sleeve.

"I went to the fights," I told him.

He shuddered. "Why don't you close the window, Jordan?"

"All right. And you should have seen what Matt did to a sailor . . .!"

He glanced at the other bed. "Is your uncle here tonight?"

"No!" I explained. "He's in hospital. Hey, I've got some clean singlets and you can have my dressing-gown."

I slid across the room and got them while Joseph peeled away his pyjama jacket and high-stepped out of the pants. In a short time he was sitting on my bed still shivering but mainly from the deliciousness of new warmth and the sound of the rain. His head was bowed, and he knotted and unknotted the tassels on the rug so raptly that it was clear he would not be diverted by Leichhardt Stadium and the sailor's eyebrow.

"Why did you want to see me?" I asked him. "It's raining like — like hell."

He sneezed again, wearily, without resistance.

"Hey, watch out! You'll have my mother out here seeing if I'm uncovered."

"That bur-luddy grenade!" he moaned.

"The grenade?"

"Yes."

"What's happened?"

A truck whined into Deakin Street. Its unhooded lights raked the ceiling and drenched Joseph with light. We listened to it shuffling up through the rain, an oil drum or two bumping on the back of it.

"He's put it all together!"

"The Comrade?"

"Yes. He came home tonight and Hilda and him were fighting. It woke me up. Then it woke Lennie. Hilda was crying so we went out into the lounge-room and he had the grenade sitting up on a dinner-plate, all put together."

"The pin and all?"

"Yes."

"Is it still all together?"

"Yes."

I could feel some terror nerve thudding in my throat.

"He said that he might as well pull out the pin and blow us all up because no one loved him and we were poor and I was a cripple. We were all crying and asking him not to. I sort of knew he wouldn't blow us up but I couldn't help crying. All he had to do was pull out that little pin."

"What happened then?"

But for that everlasting light from the railway, it was very dark now. All I could see of Joseph was the shape of his head. I heard him swallowing and sobbing intermittently.

"He just fell asleep. And Hilda took him to bed and we went back to bed too. But I was scared. I don't like thinking about that grenade all put together. I'd rather be in here."

It was easy to imagine the Comrade, wandering through the night, bound for the lavatory, pausing at the grenade, drawing the pin, leering for four fretful seconds, then dying of perversity. I could picture as well, my hands writhing to do it, how easily that small white detonator could be plucked out and the grenade rendered safe.

104

"And where did he leave that grenade when he went to bed?"

"It's still on the cabinet. I'm not game to touch it. It's on the dinner plate on the cabinet."

We listened. Perhaps through the dark walls and the rain we could hear its deadly little heart-beat.

"The trouble is," Joseph continued, "he'll wake up in the morning and blame me or Lennie or Hilda for putting it there."

"Why?"

"He doesn't remember. He doesn't remember what happens of a night." Joseph punched once sharply at the mattress. "That bur-luddy grenade," he whispered again, convinced that it was the inanimate mechanism of rods and levers and metal and amatol which had corrupted the animate Comrade.

"I know how to make it safe," I promised him. "It's easy if the Comrade really doesn't remember anything in the morning. I'd just have to take out that little white thing."

I blinked at the glittering simplicity of a new idea.

"I could just throw away the fuse. And then the grenade'd never be any good."

Joseph wagged his head very irritably, being a boy who needed sleep to loosen those diseased and gangling limbs and who was now close to exhaustion.

"No! That won't work. He'll raise old Harry in the morning if any part of that grenade is missing."

I nodded, sad at a world where simple saving ideas were blocked by equally simple damning ones. Yet it was still an achingly easy thing to creep down the Mantles' lane, with Joseph's help to make safe the grenade, the Mantles' place, our place. Then one could run back through the rain and sleep in genuinely secure warmth.

"As long as the Comrade won't remember!" I repeated.

"As long as everything's still there in the morning!" Joseph countered reverently. "As long as when he asks me, Joseph Mantle, where's that damn whadyacallit fuse, I can say, over there on that dresser. I wouldn't mind you pulling out that fuse, Jordan. But how do I know you won't blow up the whole damned street?"

"Matt taught me grenades backwards!" Getting peevish too, I defied him to believe otherwise. "Look, you start off with a pair of tweezers — you know, bathroom tweezers. Blow it all, we've got a pair in the bathroom. Then you unscrew the plug at the bottom" (if the Comrade hadn't wound it in too tightly) "and pull out the fuse with the tweezers. Even if the Comrade does pull out the pin then, it won't go off if the fuse is out. And he'll be too groggy to know what's happened."

"What do you mean groggy?" Joseph growled, but there was something merely habitual in the protest.

"What do you think I mean? I'm not going to have a blue with you over that now. He'll be too blasted groggy and you know it. He'll be too groggy to look for the fuse in the dark. So he'll just go back to bed. And then, in the morning, when he's sober, he won't want to blow himself up anyhow."

I waited as the rain cut its voice by half in the space of a second, and stopped altogether in the next two or three. There was left a gaping silence into which somebody's faulty guttering dripped resoundingly. If Joseph left me, I thought, I might lie down in the silence, whisper the Acts Eucheria had taught us, wait for the judgment day boom of the grenade. It might not kill the Jordans with any sort of pity; it might merely shatter all our windows, and start a fire in the ruins of the Mantles' place, and throw up their sundered bodies in our sight. If he left me, I might go bawling the truth to Stell. But if he wanted me to, I would go with him, balancing terror against the exultation of controlling death by means of a pair of tweezers and a twist of the hand.

"As long as you're sure the Comrade won't remember," I said once again.

"Come on!" He jumped off the bed and sought on the floor for his soaked pyjamas. Some unlikely stimulant had stirred him in the darkness. Now he wanted to rush through the whole affair and get at last to bed.

"Wait there a bit. We've got to get those tweezers. And I nearly forgot. We'll need a torch."

"Bloody oath!" Joseph murmured, a small prayer that courage and colour might be added to our perils now.

From the bathroom, I could hear the mingled breathing of Pat and my mother sleeping in the front room. I stood on the bath tub and with one knee on the wash basin, opened the shaving cabinet. Taught by the occasions when I'd come to the bathroom to have splinters pulled from various parts of me, I knew that the tweezers were on the bottom shelf. I had them in my hand and was jumping down when my knee knocked into the sink my father's shaving mug, kept there as a memorial. It spun and clattered on the porcelain. It had been made for such times, made not to break.

"Who's there?" Stell called.

"I'm just going to the toilet, love." It flattered her to call her *love*.

"Oh!"

I pushed back the toilet seat, stood straining my stomach muscles with audible success.

"I'll come and tuck you in," she offered.

"No, it's all right."

"Urrh!" said Pat, turning over.

"See you!" I whispered and returned to Joseph.

It was hard to get the window up without the covering noise of the rain. Only the slightest of winds spun along the embankment, yet the cold sawed through the place where my pyjama coat was done up, and nuzzled at my ankles. I had gumboots on, but Joseph's feet, bare on the cement paths of Deakin Street, must have been throbbing with cold.

We could not safely open the Mantles' raucous gate. Instead there was the fence. Joseph, stuffing his pyjamas into my dressing-gown pockets, slid over it first, dropping on to his hands and knees on the wet grass quite soundlessly. I vaulted it, coming down on one leg, jolting my lower and upper jaws together with an explosive snap.

"Cut it out!" Joseph grunted.

The Mantle laneway was navigable enough. There were pools of water and rowdy little pieces of gravel, but the Comrade and Hilda had no window opening on it. In the lane was utter night. We found Joseph's window, which was Lennie's also, by feel. Joseph pushed open a small fly-window that gave on to his bed.

"Oh, hell!" I stamped.

"What's the matter?"

"I didn't bring a torch!"

"I'll get you one. Do you want to come in?"

"No. You go in and you can pass things to me through the window."

"You're windy, Danny!"

"Hurry up!"

"You're windy! Give me a lift!"

I cupped my hands above my knee, and into them he

108

put his clammy foot and slid through the window. Within the limits of his fate he was very lithe.

"Won't be long," he called, and his bed creaked. Back in his own home, he was savouring the occasion. The fly-window whispered forward a few inches. By now I could just make it out.

"Are you still there?" I whispered to it, and it withdrew and no one answered.

"Oh, angel of God my guardian dear," I said. It was the bluer darkness at the end of the lane which I could not stop myself from looking at. "What side of you is your guardian angel on?" some girl in row one had asked Eucheria. And Eucheria had answered, "Your guardian angel is not on your left or on your right. He is always with you, but he does not take up earthly space as you and I do, as your mother and father and all your friends do." As the Comrade might do in the next instant at the end of the lane, giving its fourth wall of blackness beneath a moonless heaven.

Rain scampered once like mice across the roof, then slanted down in earnest. But in the narrow lane you could keep dry by pressing up against the brick, forgetting the caterpillars and the enamelled black heads of scorpions you'd seen poking out of holes in the mortar in summertime.

"To whom God's love commits me here, ever this night . . ."

"Hey, Jordan, where are you?" Joseph called lightly from the window.

"Here! Got a torch?"

"Yes. Hang on! First of all . . ."

Though the window his hands sought mine and dropped into them the grenade, greasy, cold, very heavy. The little finger of my right hand could feel the edge of the plug, and I arranged my hands around the surface and tried to unscrew it. As I ground my teeth, Joseph turned a very sick torchlight on my efforts.

For over a minute I strained at the plug, in darkness again because Joseph had decided that even that sparse light was unnecessary. Without my even knowing that he had gone, he came back from the kitchen where the Comrade kept, hung from the gas-pipe as if he were a most avid handyman, a hammer, a wrench, a spirit level, and a few other basic tools.

"Here are some pliers," he whispered, shining the torch on them.

Within a short time the pliers had done their work, Joseph grasping the grenade, the torch tucked under his arm and spraying the lane with dim drunken light as we writhed over the plug. When we had it out, I dropped it into my pyjama coat pocket and drew out the tweezers.

Their silver arms were on the belly of the fuse as Joseph's torch snapped off.

"Don't move!" he said.

From the front of the house came a wail that might have been a motorbike far up Deakin Street at first, but mounted to become the shriek of a man falling down some chasm. The grenade flew from my hands like a frog. I did not hear it fall, my ears drenched with that unchecked screeching. At length, we could hear Hilda's voice, hushing, dissipating the noise.

"It's all right. It's all right, dear. Settle down. Nothing's happening. I'm with you."

"It's just the Comrade," Joseph explained. "He has nightmares."

I knelt immediately among the puddles, seeking the grenade with my hands before Azrail, angel of death, could plummet down and give it a final explosive kick. The knees of my pyjamas became wet and muddied. It would be the morning's job to explain that to Stell, as, if morning ever came, I'd be willing to.

"Give us a bit of torch!" I begged Joseph.

He swept the floor of the lane with light. Lolled in a quarter of an inch of slush was the grenade. Since it was best to deal with it where it lay, I remained kneeling, tilting it towards me, and did as I had promised Joseph — plucked out the detonator. When I had the plug back in, I wiped the whole thing clean with my pyjama coat.

"Here you are!"

I pushed the grenade and detonator at him through the window.

"Come on, give me back my dressing-gown."

"You're in a blasted hurry," he commented, but eventually he passed it out to me. I made a cape of it around my shoulders.

"Goodnight!"

I ran off lightly, all but blind in the rain. Let the Comrade hear a gumboot squash into a puddle! My cold joints worked like a racehorse's. Over the Comrade's fence, and I was thinking of the pyjamas. I could postpone discovery of them until the next washing day by putting them deep into the dirty clothes bag and dressing in my other pair.

It seemed that the drugged sleepiness of the bedroom returned instantly to me, with the window locked and the rain gurgling beyond it. The pyjamas managed to get themselves changed; and since I was convinced in an obscure way that I had offended someone of importance, I made an act of contrition. That and a luxurious instant or two of warmth are my last memories of an improperly long night.

14

Sunday had been a depressing, safe day, padded in on all sides by soaking rain. No sound, not even of a raised voice, came from the Mantles'. Traffic on the highway hummed on a long uniform note which became a mere refinement of silence, and most of the day's trains, with their airbrakes on, seethed past dully on the wet rails.

Pat made no concession to the weather. Like a demoniac Judy Garland, she waltzed from chore to chore. She was a loud, gay girl as she peeled the spuds, for Noel had been asked to dinner.

For me it was a limp, vaguely guilty day, and every old idea I picked up and fingered flashed back its agate edge of guilt. Provoked by the rain, I thought of sleep and warmth, the times I had felt them advancing like companionable mists filling up the valley bottoms. But uneasiness for last night's lack of them prevailed. I thought of escapade, of Sundays at the old wharf on our river up north. We would sway on it until its rotten timbers swayed also. At one time, one of my friends crashed through its planking (cut by men dead fifty years before) and dropped into waist-deep silt across which a panic-ridden black snake slithered for the bank.

But last night's humourless sabotage had soured all that.

In the afternoon we visited Matt in hospital. He snuffled at us unfamiliarly through a white mask which covered half his face. He was well enough though, pinching all the nurses' backsides for our scandal and amusement. But not even Matt could make it a day worth the living.

Beneath Monday's honest sun sopping up the dew, I crossed the railway bridge to the bus. It seemed that above us was a new universe dwelt in by homelier fates. Under them, I was confident that normality could be conjured back to Deakin Street. I yearned to get to Eucheria and become involved in the endless Monday lessons, to utter them as a propitiation. For there were omens and prodigies beginning to unhinge my life, and the repetition of ordinary things would be a spell against them.

For most of the morning, I managed to be half-happy and welcomed tedium as an opiate. The hours washed over me like the tide over the home of a shellfish who feels that if he can keep his purchase on the sand for a while longer, he will be secure for ever.

Eucheria herself destroyed the oblivion of the morning by telling at half past eleven a story which, considering that memorable day as a whole, it has always been impossible to forget. Years afterwards, in a classical Greek class, I recognised the names of the two lovers of Eucheria's story with the same shrill an Englishman in the Siberian *taiga* might feel if he came on an inn owned by a Brown or an O'Toole.

There was a prince called Soter, Eucheria told us, who had always lived in his father the King's citadel built of the world's best cedar, marble and gold on a hill above an ancient town. Soter had never left this home, had never needed or wished to. He could remember no other life.

When he was still a young man, he heard one evening, drifting up the hill with the smoke from the town's fires, the spellbinding voice of a young lady singing for the townspeople after their day's work. From the time he first heard the voice, Soter knew that he could not leave this young woman to perish amongst the diseases and poverty which had spoilt the beauty of the town.

One twilight when he waited on the walls listening to her, he filled his lungs with the evening air, and himself began to sing. His voice spread over the town like a honey-brown cloud, fell on its roofs like a sweet rain. In his song, the prince pleaded with the girl to leave the squalid streets and climb the narrow ridge to the palace gate, where they could, for the first time and for at least a few seconds, see each other's splendour.

For a long time there was silence in the town which had heard its prince and the princely power of his voice. The girl was the first to speak, in an undertone, asking some of the townsmen to lead her up the defile to her lord. One by one, in voices coarser by the second, they refused. They would not give up their songstress even to Soter. She would have to stay below the hill like themselves, suffering the same ugliness, hunger, fatigue and death as they would. On the wall, the sense of loss shook Soter's body.

In the town, the crowds broke up. The girl limped home, no spirit left for singing. Soter, who could see the whole town laid out below him like a map, thought that there was something questing and wary about her as she moved along the streets, her hands stretched a little way ahead of her. He watched each step she took, so closely, so affectionately, that it was some time before he saw that she had come to the edge of the town. With an early moon glittering on the outline of her hair, she had begun to mount the hill. Some of the people saw this from their windows and ran out to stop her, but when they saw their prince on the walls, they went back home.

Yet the girl seemed unable to deal with that steep climb in the quarter-light. Soon she fell over a boulder and lay weeping. Blood flowed from a gash on her forehead. Weak with pity, Soter clutched the cold stone of the ramparts.

"Tell me what your name is," he called to her, "and why you cannot climb this hill."

"My name is Pneuma," she called back. "And I cannot climb this hill because I am blind."

Soter staggered back from the walls. Except for his father, he had never known such love as he knew then. For no one had he ever known such tenderness.

"Go back to your home for this short night, Pneuma," he said. "Tomorrow I shall send a palace guard to guide you along the ridge. From tomorrow's dawn you will live in my house and be the glory of the King's family."

Soter stood on the wall all through the night with the dew on his hair and mists gathering around him. At dawn he sent the Captain of the Guard down into the town to find Pneuma. But when the royal officer asked the townspeople where she lived, they stoned him, and drove him back up the ridge. It was a sick and bleeding Captain of the Guard who reported to Soter without having even seen the girl.

Beneath the morning sun, Soter gazed down on the stirring town and yearned to see Pneuma. From a palace window came the moans of the Captain as the King's physicians tended him. It was no use sending soldiers for the girl, Soter decided. He would go himself. The idea came to him with a rush, and he ran to tell the King.

The King listened to him and approved the project. "But," he said, "as long as she is blind, how can she choose between the squalor of the town and the grandeur of the palace? In this small casket" — and he drew from a pocket within his royal robes a box cut from a single lump of onyx — "is the gift of sight. Its casket might as well be onyx as gold, for there is no fit home for it on this earth other than the kingly head of man. Give this gift to Pneuma in the hope that she will climb this mountain to reign with us of her own free accord. Only then will she be welcome at my court."

In the town, carrying the casket concealed, Soter was not recognised. The people did not expect him to have come down to them, to be walking the littered, ill-drained streets. Within a sort time, he reached Pneuma's home and saw her rise swaying with delight at the sound of his voice.

"Pneuma, I have not come to take you to my father's house," he told her. "I have come to give you the gift of sight so that whenever you wish you can freely come to me, and just as freely leave again."

"If I could see all the kingdoms," she told him, "and all the towns that have been and will be, I would still never leave you for an instant."

He took out the gift, and Pneuma waited, breathless in the darkness which she had known from her first baby breath. But the onyx box could not be opened, though Soter pulled at it from every side and hurled it against the walls of Pneuma's home in the hope of breaking it and dashing the gift into the girl's eyes. In the end, Pneuma wept softly and slumped to the dirt floor, crippled with despair.

The townspeople, hearing Soter's frenzied efforts to crack the onyx box, collected before the girl's house, and at last recognised the prince. In the crowd was a young labourer who would not give up his hopes of Pneuma's love, not even for the King's son. He inflamed this crowd of people who did not want to lose their songstress, inflamed them to such a fury of resentment against Soter that they crowded into Pneuma's hovel screaming their hate in Soter's face, ripping the royal emblems from his clothing, spitting on his noble brow, flinging at him blow after blow until he fell, and kicking his royal body until he was on the edge of death. Then the young labourer came forward to Soter and, with his knife, dug out the prince's eyes.

When the crowd saw this last enormity, they rushed away to their homes. Their shame they hid behind locked doors and boarded windows; but there was no way to block their ears against the wailing of Pneuma bent across the shattered body of her prince.

Yet, in her blindness, her hand stumbled on the onyx box. Now she tried to open it and give him the benefit of whatever lay inside. Soter's blood had drenched it, and now it opened to a flick of her hand. She felt for the gift, lifting it out of the casket. It was a real thing but neither round nor square, soft nor hard, heavy nor light. It had the feel of being infinitely precious, and when she had lifted it a little way, it melted through her hands like water. In the following instant, she knew for the first time what it was to see, for she saw the bloodied face of her lord, and, even as it was, it was the most piteous and beautiful thing she was ever to see. In the strength of her love, in the clearness of her vision, no one daring to stand in her way, the young labourer having darkened his house and locked himself in raving with guilt, she carried Soter back to his father's house, where her love and the King's power restored his sight and his strength completely.

In their kingdom on the hill, Pneuma became Soter's queen.

Of course, said Sister Eucheria, Soter is the Saviour and Pneuma is the Soul of Man, blinded by the Fall, unable to find its way to the Kingdom, until the Saviour came down from His Father's House to give it the chance of returning freely with him. But the gift he brought could be opened only by his blood, just as the onyx box was opened by Soter's blood. And as by that gift Pneuma was strong and able to carry Soter's bleeding body, the Soul of Man became strong, became pure, pure enough to carry the bleeding body of the Lord in his own body. As we would soon do, said Eucheria, when we approached the mystery of Christ's Body and Blood.

In the classroom there was only the sound of breathing, every mind dabbling for implications in Eucheria's story. Yet allegories are, in more than one way, delusive. Even on that Monday I sensed this, that in Eucheria's class, beneath the smooth faces were personalities already jagged and motives already intricate. The grand simplicity, the single purposeness of people like Soter and Pneuma had almost vanished even here. Except in the cases of Dolph Conlon and Sister Eucheria. But these were rarities; and Eucheria was the story-teller and therefore, in some strange way, did not come into account.

So, as I listened to the story, unaware as yet of what it symbolised, I found myself gazing across at Dolph. He was sniffling sadly with his head sideways on his blazer shoulder, and only his fear that he would not be able to pull out his handkerchief in time holding back from complete absorption. Gwen Callan and the Lilies of Sharon did not glance in his humble direction — four seats down in row four. Each of them confidently saw herself as Pneuma. But I stared at Dolph, not because he was identifiable in the story, but because, take away his leaky nose, he was simply straightforward enough to inhabit the same honest world as Soter.

It *was* an honest world, I thought, in a multiplicity of ways. It was a grandly untechnical world. To have his way with Pneuma, the young labourer had to win a crowd. To crush Soter's bones he had to wield his own fist, ply his own boot. To blind Soter he had to clutch his own knife, and suffer the guilty mess on his own hands. He could not destroy his enemy from an antiseptic distance. In that world you had to do your own searing, rending, breaking, blinding. You could not simply draw a pin, hurl a mechanism, pull down your hat and walk away.

A small girl from third class tottered down the corridor jangling the dinnertime handbell. We said grace and stood like statues, the row that most successfully stood like statues being let out first. One row held their breaths for so long and hunched up their shoulders so crookedly that no sculptor would have admitted to them. Yet Eucheria usually let them go first.

When I intercepted Dolph, he was dawdling across the asphalt on his own. I led him away to the bench furthest from the incinerator, where all the master spirits seemed to be. We sat and opened our bundles of sandwiches in that quiet corner where the sun had shone all morning. The brick wall warmed our backs through our clothes. Dolph bent his pale, freckled face to his food, ruminated on it with his thick Irish eyebrows. A face of no great account, I thought, but brave enough and definitely stubborn. Eucheria didn't send him on messages to other nuns, but that was probably because she didn't want mucus all over her envelopes. Anyhow, I told him the entire history of the Comrade's grenade.

119

I told him how it had been, according to the state of the Comrade's liver, set aside for the Conlons' destruction, for the destruction of the Mantles themselves, and might, next time the Comrade was drunk or angry, be dedicated to anyone, even to the Jordans. At first, Dolph cried very quietly to avoid drawing the attention of one of those ten-year-old girl prefects. He could see that if the Comrade could abstain from pulling the pin on his own family while suicidal with booze, the night would come when he'd pull it on the Conlons and fling it through their lounge-room windows.

My friend composed himself by taking a few fierce bites from his sandwich. Now he began to threaten that he'd tell his father who'd tell the police. But the Comrade would blame it all on me, I protested. Dolph swore that my name as the source of the story would be kept a secret; and one promise of Dolph's would outlast a gross of Lennie's. My underlids quivered with joy. From under my eyeballs a few warm tears rolled up. I was aware of the sun glinting on them. Now all the weight of the business was on the Conlons.

But Dolph entered a third stage of defiance.

"If you know how grenades work," he said, "then why don't we blow it up ourselves?" His face had already pinkened with rage. He was consumed with a mature anger at the Comrade's having introduced such an untoward element into our lives; an anger which I felt only hazily and at times, since I still thought that adults, guided by esoteric motives, had the right to be as inhuman as they liked.

"I'd rather do that," Dolph growled. "I'd rather blow up that old dill's bomb all by myself. Will you, Danny?"

"We wouldn't be able to get it. Listen, Dolph, how would we get it? We can't steal it out of his place." I still felt securer than I had been for days, but Dolph's features were bunched in the most intractable of frowns.

"You'd better just tell your father about it," I prompted.

"I'd rather blow it up myself. To pay him back quits. Anyhow, can't you ask Joseph to get at it for you?"

It was true that Joseph would be willing to be rid of the grenade which had had malicious influence on his father.

"What if we just got it and threw it in the Parramatta River?" I suggested.

Dolph shook his head over some minute point of honour.

"That wouldn't be paying him back quits."

I began to dislike the term.

"The Comrade would *pay me back quits* if he found his grenade was gone."

As an expression of anguish, I re-wrapped my lunch. In a world of want, we were forbidden to throw food away in the playground. I would have to take it home with me or fling it into some vacant allotment between school and the railway.

"I'll tell you what," Dolph said. "My father comes home from work about the middle of the night. They call his shift the middle shift. Then he has a bath. You ought to hear our bath-heater going. It wakes Robert up." (Robert was his elder brother.) "A lot of the time it wakes me up. I'll make sure it wakes me up tonight."

"How can you be sure something'll wake you up?" I asked irritably.

"I'll make sure. Look, Danny, let's show him! Let's show him we think he's an old fool!"

Some years later, when Dolph's father came to sue a national trade union before the High Court of Australia, it was demonstrated even once more that out

121

of a strange, doomed perversity, Conlons would bow only to an enemy smaller, more defenceless than themselves. For a little time, no more than fifteen seconds, Dolph's wish to *show* the Comrade presented itself to me as what decency irresistibly demanded.

"But the Comrade," I whispered. "If he ever found out!"

Dolph was eating quickly, his perturbation no longer fear but something healthier. It demanded that he should be nourished.

"I'll tell you what!" he said. You could see that he was trying to balance sense and honour, if sense is the word for my side of the argument. As he spoke, he gauged me from under his thick farmer-like eyebrows. When the bath-heater woke him that night, he would come and wake me. We would then get the grenade . . .

"How?"

"Can't you work it out with Joseph?" He spoke patiently, yet as if he had every right to be impatient. I too felt that he did. "Didn't you say he hated that grenade?" he asked.

Therefore we would wake Joseph, take the grenade to the swamps, a partly reclaimed wasteland by the river, and explode the thing. There was no other possible way to *show* the Comrade. Dolph was profoundly convinced of that. Whenever it was that we got back from the swamps, that was time to tell Mr Conlon or the police or any other adult agency; and Dolph promised to call on all of them as soon as we did return.

"It'd be the bravest adventure of all," Dolph decided. "It'd be marvellous!"

It would be the sort of endeavour that justified the food a person ate. In the dark with Dolph, to hurl that detested thing away. Far away in Deakin Street, the

Comrade might hear it in his sleep and stir screaming.

"It'd certainly show him," I conceded.

15

With a feeling that I had come a great way towards spiting the Comrade, I made my arrangements with Joseph. But when night came, the dream of defiance sufficed, as I believed it would suffice for Dolph and Joseph. I was gay at table, and Stell, who had looked sideways at my recent pale cast of thought, sent me to bed with a lot of hugging.

When Dolph knocked on my window, as on a front door, I woke choleric, muttering uselessly at the closed pane. The air was full of a seething which at first I thought was a locomotive sidling along the embankment. It was in fact a great wind, and Deakin Street, which was a street of few trees, seemed that night to be raving with leaves. Wind cuffed brick corners, and chased its tail on little landings and in the courtyards of flats. The world was unreasonably cold, unreasonably late, unreasonably stubborn in the wispy figure of Dolph who could be barely seen, waiting for me beneath a lemon tree which overhung our place on the east.

When I'd asked him about the grenade that afternoon, Joseph had been very sanguine. To him, the films were an infinite source of useful expedients. Abandoned in any part of the earth and in any circumstances, he would never have despaired until he had tried the last item in his sizeable corpus of Hollywood veldtcraft. All that was needed tonight was a quick, quiet means of waking him, but whatever it was, it would have to be based on something he'd seen at the Mercury on Saturday afternoons. Finally, he decided to knot lengths of string together, tie one end around his thumb, have the other end trailing free from his bedroom window.

The Mantles' side gate was open for us, and grinding softly in the wind. The lane was not as black as it had been two nights before, and we found the string swaying through the barely opened window and pulled it. There was a soft unprotesting gurgle. Within seconds the grenade was handed through to us, followed by the detonator, followed by Joseph's long legs questing firm ground.

In Deakin Street it was dark but for the few hooded lights from the signal box and station. In the north-east was a nearly full moon, but the wind seemed to blur its influence. The time was probably after one o'clock. The houses mouldered dully, tucked away behind their gardens like the handicraft of people long since called away. The highway was empty. On our way back there might be fruit shop people driving in early to the city markets. But this was too early even for them.

Dolph and Joseph seemed to move together very companionably for people who had scarcely met before. "You didn't take long to get ready," Dolph complimented Joseph. "I slept in my clothes," Joseph explained, pulling his crumpled collar up around his ears. His pants hung crookedly, over one hip, under the other.

As for the grenade, which I was bearing clutched in against my stomach, it had for two days sat up on the dinner plate where it had been left on Saturday night. Joseph had put the detonator behind some letters on the smaller cabinet but, as far as the Comrade knew, his little green pudding of death had been fully primed all Sunday and Monday. A significant listlessness had overcome the Comrade since his return. Or perhaps he had brought it home with him from his sojourn with the orange crêpe lady. Neighbours had been outraged on two occasions to see him slumped against his far fence, not bothering at need to move the five yards to his lavatory, but urinating in full sight of them. They had reported the fact to each other as if it were proof of ultimate decacy. They did not know about the grenade.

Just off the highway, the Meatpackers, the Glasgow Arms' rival, waited in dim green tile, humping a long and shaky upstairs veranda. It was a sad, amicable old pub with suspect refrigeration. Bred in the days of blither licensing laws, the few mad hours of dyspeptic carouse allowed in 1942 tired it. It had that same air you saw in matrons nodding their heads over coupon-books. The Meatpackers knew what it was to suffer the whimsies of legislators.

We were nearly past it when someone called to Joseph from the other side of the highway. The wind distorted the call, enough to justify us in hiding in the Saloon Bar entrance. Against the cold bitter smell of disinfected steps, we held our breath. Now that we had begun our undertaking, we wanted it attended by the conventional hazards and alarms. Yet before we even glanced into the open street, we knew that it was merely Lennie pursuing us.

I had never felt such pity for him as then. He was scampering over the highway, chased by all the phantoms of his six and a half years on this earth. He did not look back over his shoulder at them, but from side to side, seeming embarrassed, not wanting to be seen by anyone but us. He considered himself unmanfully dressed. As the three of us moved spontaneously out of the shadows to show him where we were, he hurried up carrying his short pants by their firemen's braces with his sandshoes in his other hand. His feet were bare beneath his pyjama trousers and he had a cardigan on over his pyjama coat.

"Wait till *you* want to go somewhere!" he threatened Joseph.

"This is very dangerous," Joseph explained calmly. "I didn't want you to get killed."

"Well, wait for me now!" he demanded.

He charged in the doorway of the Meatpackers and Joseph did up his shoe-laces. Benumbed that our enterprise had brought us as far as the far side of the highway, we accepted Lennie as a partner to it. For who could drag him caterwauling round to Deakin Street and put him back to bed? Sitting on the steps, he sneezed three joyous, abandoned sneezes.

"My colonial!" he told us sunnily. "I'm glad I caught up to you."

We went on. The wind kept us quiet, blowing what we said down the road as irretrievably as a fat man's bowler. The grenade was warm on the side against my stomach while my fingers, cupped around its outer side, were numbed so that it felt strangely unequal in shape. When the cement footpaths gave way to grass we walked processionally. Beyond the last house, on the edge of the swamps, Joseph demanded a rest. We sat in a circle on the damp earth while he took off his shoes and massaged the balls of his feet.

"Does it hurt much?" Dolph asked.

"Not too much," Joseph sighed.

His little brother spat or made the noise of spitting. "He's only going to die of it, that's all!"

"When?"

"Hilda . . . she's my mother," Joseph told Dolph, "her young brother died of it when he was sixteen."

"That's not too bad," Dolph said. "That's a long while yet. You can have a lot of . . . of fun . . . before then."

Lennie persisted. "He gets terrible pains."

"I had a cousin called Peewee Conlon. Everyone called him Peewee. He drank kerosene and died when he was four. That was unlucky. Anyhow, you might live longer than all of us."

Dolph was not a liar, even by intonation. He was giving comfort, and you could tell he was merely giving comfort. On the damp verge of the swamp our foal blood stirred against the worm of death even as he spoke. No merely doctrinal training could convince us that it was a blessed thing to die young. Only Joseph, who had always carried his doom intravenously, was unaffected by the sharp taste of death which alighted for a second on our lips like a fly, and was then blown away. Joseph gave his feet a final knead and put his shoes back on.

We went on for over a mile along a gravel road lined by briary scrub. This hissed and crackled like a brush fire as the wind combed it about. A few miles away, across the darkling salt flats, two radio towers rose iridescent to the moon. Joseph pointed to them.

"The one closest to us has *Rip Ramrod and the Plainsman*."

"Boy, did he fix the Cattle Baron!" breathed Lennie.

"And that other one is the one *Guns Gatsby's* on."

"We're allowed to listen to *Guns Gatsby*," Dolph

said. "But *Rip Ramrod's* on at the same time as the ABC news."

"Urrh!" we grunted.

Now there was an embankment on our left, and beyond it a gradual basin where antique bedsteads, depleted batteries, cracked cylinder-heads, disembowelled mattresses, corroding chamber pots decayed in a tangle.

"Where are we going to blow the thing up?" Joseph asked, implying that this was the place. I agreed. We could hurl the grenade into the tip and shelter beneath the embankment. Lennie nodded. "Yes!" said Dolph.

At my shoulder, Lennie sniffled heavily while, with Dolph playing torchlight on my hands, and Joseph holding the grenade, I performed the insertion of the detonator. Someone whistled at my adroitness and I poked at the small white fuse once again, frowning at the same doubt which I had suffered at Joseph's baptism. This purely adult thing, a special weapon of destruction, seemed improperly easy of operation. I screwed in the plug and we all in turn gave it a final tightening. I smiled.

"Rightoh! It's ready. Don't worry if I drop it. We dropped it the other night, didn't we, Joseph? And it didn't go off."

We climbed the bank. Below us in a jumbled mess whose silhouette we could hardly make out were the mean relics of a thousand lives, soon to be joined by a relic of the frenzies and fears of the Comrade. We were exposed now from head to heels to the wind, from the quarter of the Tower which broadcast *Rip Ramrod and the Plainsman*. It butted us in the small of our backs. It boxed our ears and made as if to scalp us.

"When I pull this out" — and I pointed to the pin — "and let the grenade go, we've got four seconds." They would have to hug the embankment with their hands over their ears.

"Can you throw it far enough?" Dolph asked mildly.

"Of course I can."

"I think the one who can throw the furthest ought to throw it." Joseph dropped on his haunches and searched the ground. "Why don't we have a try-out with a goolie?"

So we had a confused throwing trial along the length of the embankment which Dolph won. Throughout the contest the grenade had lain beside the torch on top of Lennie's pyjama pants. Now I picked it up and tipped it into Dolph's cupped hands.

"It's heavy," he whispered in reverence. "I can't throw this far enough."

"Then why the hell did you kick up a fuss in the first place?"

Dolph shrugged. "I didn't want to start a blasted fight."

"We should have stayed at home in bed." As a comment on our indecision, Joseph sat down on a nearby kerosene drum.

"Why don't we throw it in this can," he said without warning, "and roll the can down the slope? It'd go further than we can ever fling it."

I grunted at his typically exotic idea. "Give the damn thing to me. I'll hoy it far enough for you."

"Wait a bit!" Lennie said. "It's the Mantles' grenade. Don't forget that!"

It was a point. On its basis, Joseph reiterated, "I reckon chuck the grenade in the can and roll the can down to all that rubbish."

Dolph noddely urbanely. "I reckon that's a good idea. Here you are, Danny."

My hands received the grenade again and Dolph went

and dragged the drum into place. As he turned it, the wind bassooned against its lip. Lennie giggled at the sound. We waited while Joseph tried to argue his brother into taking shelter behind the mound. But Lennie claimed he had come especially to see the pin drawn. His small face, blue under the moon, opposed us like a shut fist. Not that there was cause for argument. A few strides would take us all into safety.

Dolph bent to the can, ready to roll it downhill.

"Ready?" he said as if the words were a large lie or a sacrament, whose effects would never be wiped out.

I clutched the orb with both hands and Joseph pulled the pin. We loitered in that awesome moment when death had only the sinews of my thumbs to beat.

"When I throw this in the case, run!"

It was thrown and the can began to roll, but not one of them ran. We were hip to hip with death, yet so safe; and the rareness of our situation imposed on us its own inertia. The can rolled smoothly for a second, but snagged to a stop on a half-buried beer-bottle or a contrary scrub root. Moving to it, Dolph tried to kick it along with the sole of his foot. There was an echo of heroism to the metal clip of his shoe striking the metal of the drum. Lennie did not resist rushing forward and lunging with his sandshoe.

"Come on," I yelled, and turning, careered into Joseph. We dragged each other down into safety, but the Comrade's grenade went off before we got our hands to our ears. The noise snatched the breath out of our mouths. Air gathered, bulged, cracked open like a watermelon. Reverberations wailed away down the road, stumbled off through the scrub. Silence came when the embankment fell in and half-buried us.

We struggled out of the damp soil and ran through a hardly altered landscape to Dolph and Lennie. Dolph was on his stomach, with his head towards us, his backside in the air and his knees pushed hard up under his stomach. His body seemed whole until I laid my ear down on his back to listen for his heart or the rattle of breath. I found myself staring into a large irregular wound in the back of his head and, at the same instant, tepid blood welled from a place between his shoulders and wet the side of my face. It was useless to listen for a noise in his body, what with ringing ears and the wind yelling at my shoulder.

Lennie was on his back, with his head closer to the place of the blast. Joseph knelt over him silently, and it was Lennie who sobbed briefly, so softly that you couldn't swear to it. Some sizable piece, perhaps the plug, had shorn away the left side of his face from the eye down. My head was clearer now and I put my ear to his heart. There was no sound.

"Hell, Joseph," I moaned. "Hell, we've killed the two of them."

Joseph looked up from the hideous face, and then slumped to lie beside his brother.

"That bur-luddy grenade!" he told me. "That bur-luddy grenade!"

16

Dr Slattery injected something into Joseph's hip and mine, and whatever it was, it held me for seven or eight hours a whit below the surface of sleep. Here imagination and memory moiled imperfectly around the images of Lennie and Dolph. There was daylight on my eyelids, but Dr Slattery's alchemy kept them shut, and in the funereal yellowness of that morning sleep, I spoke freely with both the boys. Intermittently one of us would remember that they were dead, but the fact could not destroy our familiarity, and very soon we would be yarning again in the way we were used to.

"Victims!" said the Comrade, full of doleful reasonableness in the kitchen. The boys melted at that word. They would never be back. My eyes opened to drawn curtains and a closed door. Light like a brown light of mortuaries was in the room. Traffic was in full voice both in Deakin Street and on the highway. In the kitchen my mother and the Comrade were engaged in a dialogue amazingly temperate on the Comrade's side, amazingly frank on my mother's. It was probably the longest conversation they were ever to have with each other.

"Let me speak to you as to a reasonable man," my mother said. "You haven't been reasonable in the past. You try to get away from things by drink or bullying."

It was strange, waking to hear people talking in their wide-awake mid-morning voices.

"Hell, have you to bully a man? I've lost my son. My only healthy son. I don't blame anyone. If kids find something like that in the swamps, they'd want to blow it up. I just came in here in sorrow, to see if Daniel said anything yet."

My mother laughed at him, as mockingly as she liked. For some reason he was no more than a bad joke to her now.

"You're a poor, miserable lump. Yes, and you needn't glower at me in *my* house. You've had too free a run, Mr Red. I know about your grenade. And I know how you got it. On the black with money borrowed from a fancy lady."

The Comrade rumbled out a spiritless protest. A chair grated briefly along the floor and I realised that the Comrade was seated at the table like the best of neighbours exchanging sympathy the morning after a disaster.

"I've been in contact with my father at the Cape. Trunkline to the fishing co-op. He knows all about it now. I've posted a letter to Brian. It'll take a week or so to get there. When it arrives, Brian will know who's to blame, too."

"Why in the hell did you want to . . .?" the Comrade asked quietly.

"Because I didn't want to be found strangled in a stormwater canal. I know you, Mr Lenin. You'd end my happy life without a qualm. Just to keep on with your miserable one."

A kettle squealed. Stell called above it.

"You couldn't take a week's imprisonment, locked up from your pleasures. If ever a man needed his coarse little pleasures . . . !"

The kettle was silenced. It was probably the water for young Brian's noonday bath.

"Your liberty depends on me now, Comrade."

"For God's sake," he grunted, "you could stop calling me *Comrade* and *Mr Red*."

"Perhaps," my mother speculated. "Anyhow, I promise you nothing. Except I swear to you, before the God who brought you out of nothing — why, only He knows — that if I see you even look in Daniel's direction in the days to come, you're a finished man."

There was a slack sound of the Comrade flopping his head down on the table.

"I don't know," he groaned. "You'd never talk to me like this if I wasn't buggered with grief. And buggered with something else too. I don't know." It was a voice that longed for sleep.

"All right, then," said Stell, hard as flint. "I don't want to even lay eyes on you again. You will not look sideways. Or speak or act sideways. If I come down Deakin Street and you want to walk up it, wait till I've gone, turn back inside. No more foul eyes, Comrade, no sort of eyes at all. Remember all this, Comrade! Remember it so well that no matter how drunk you are, you'll still realise that if you come near us it's the end of you. I want you to understand too. You might be the People's fool, but I'm not the People's woman."

"All right, all right, all right!" he growled. "I'll be an angel. All I care about anyhow is Lennie. If I began to cry, if I could start crying for him, I'd never stop. But why don't you think of Joseph. Don't you think his life's been bad enough? Say there was an inquest. And then a trial. Him being asked questions that'd put his father in jail. Think of that.''

"Joseph is all I do think of. Joseph and Hilda. I think of them more than you do.''

"I must have a tumour on the brain," the Comrade claimed very softly.

"Have you ever thought you might be just rotten?" Stell had spoken breathlessly this time, as if every word were a risk. But the Comrade sighed and waited for her to go on.

"Hilda has lost her son," she said. "It was a horrible way to lose a boy. Instead of staying with her, you're roaming around trying to organise people into keeping you out of trouble. Why don't you just go home and spend the day in honest grief?"

After this, they were quiet for a long time. I feared that they had been swept away by one of those cross-currents of sorcery which derange human affairs. We had had such matters read to us, by Eucheria for instance. However, it appears that the Comrade was merely slumped over the table. At last the chair rasped as he got up.

"I think I'll go," he sighed. "I can't be bothered going and I can't be bothered staying. But a bloke has to move or they'd think he was dead. I should be angry at someone. I don't know. I saw Lennie this morning. His face was awful. Even what was left. But I can't be bothered being angry. And, don't worry, I can't be bothered bothering you. And don't be scared even if I do. I'm just a poor bastard."

He pushed out the back door and it flopped loosely shut behind him, a dead and disenchanted sound. Almost immediately, Stell opened my door and, seeing that I was awake, stumbled to me and cupped my head against her chest. She shivered for the Arctic closeness of death.

The old red-headed police sergeant grunted at Stell's question.

"It's no use asking me to be lenient for the sake of his wife. If your story's true, he's an irresponsible maniac. Nothing can save him from prosecution."

The sergeant stared into his drained tea cup. He had confessed earlier to having grandchildren, and you could see past the blue serge, nickel badges, silver braid, to the freckled semi-baldness, the scraggy neck and flabby shoulders of a grandfather.

"No," he said, "you can't save him, but let him go on thinking you might. He's pathetic as long as you've got the whiphand. But if he realised you didn't have it, well . . ."

My mother said, "Sergeant, Daniel seems to think it's his fault."

The sergeant turned to me, wrinkling his kindly freckles.

"It wasn't your fault, cobber. It was this Mantle bloke's."

He glared at me with terrible conviction, and then cast about for his hat.

The red-headed sergeant had pity on Joseph and Hilda. He could have pestered the truth from them. But he accepted the boy's statement that he had found the grenade himself, and Hilda's claim that she had heard or seen nothing about her husband's obtaining anything lethal.

The sergeant was wise in a fashion. Grief had bewildered Hilda, and she numbly pursued her habit of loyalty to the Comrade. After a week or two, she would wake in the morning and know from head to heel that

137

Lennie her son's familiar body was definitely below the ground, that for it there would never again be hugs and pay-day ice-cream and bread and treacle at half past three. That would be enough to crack any habit.

"This boy," Sister Stanislaus told her third grade, "this boy went off playing with explosives in the middle of the night. Didn't you sir?"

I agreed with her, eyes down. Someone had spilt a great quantity of ink on the floor. The stain spread on the amber lacquered boards like a continent of night, as irregular as the continents of the earth. In one of its wider gulfs I landed an invading force with my eye. It edged inland from the beaches.

"And because of this foolishness there was an accident. Wasn't there, sir? Tell the class!"

I didn't want to tell them. I dug my chin into my chest instead.

"Dolph Conlon blew himself up. Didn't he, sir?"

"Yes."

I turned my head to glance at the class. Through the mist of tears, their eyes homing on my face were enormous, but their faces no more rapt than if I'd broken a window. I felt with great joy that I had returned to them, that in weeks past or to come many of them, who had never seen or touched a grenade, had been or would be stood above that little island of ink to be intimidated by Stanislaus.

"Why did you do what you did, sir? Why did you go out in the night with a bomb in your hands?"

"Dolph wanted me to."

"Don't hide behind Dolph, sir. Dolph is with God. Would you start telling lies against one of God's saints?"

"It's the truth, Sister. Dolph wanted us to."

138

"I believe you, sir," she decided efficiently. "You're fortunate you're not with God yourself — before your time, like Dolph."

She turned to her desk, disapproved of the time she read from her large watch there, took a reading book from the bottom of a pile and gave it a spell on the top. There was a stick of green chalk on the desk which she moved six inches. Seventy eyes scoured her for the meaning of these ritual motions.

"And you wanted to save people's lives, isn't that so?"

"Yes!" By now I could scarcely force the cracked word up my throat. Grief poured from me like a malarial sweat, and I was alive again, *aware* of windows and sun and Stanislaus' brow and vast white sleeves, the blazers of the boys, the tight plaits of the girls, and the irreparable shame of bawling beyond control into a soaked handkerchief in front of so many people.

"Well, God may be satisfied with your reasons, sir. I am not. I will not have children from this school wandering in the darkness, traipsing into every kind of danger. Night-time adventures! None of you *dare*!"

The last word quivered above our heads like Damocles' sword in a breeze. Her jaw jutted abnormally wide, unchallengable, clear of her coif. She waited, considering the wisdom of her next ploy. But she knew that few children tell their parents of the more startling violences of the classroom. And it was worthy to trample on the graves of the dead for the sake of the living.

"If Dolph Conlon were here," she told me, "I would punish him as severely, Daniel Jordan, as I am now going to punish you. Helen Flanagan, bring me the feather duster."

A ceremonial little girl rose and marched to the back of the room. From a bookcase full of Blinky Bill and

Enid Blyton, she pulled a yellow feather duster with a long cane handle. Through space full of the roll of drums, she bore it to Stanislaus. It had never seen dust, and its yellow feathers came from only God knew what fantastic bird eyried on God knew what unconquered peak.

"Give me your hand, sir!"

The cane handle scorched my palm three times, singing as it came. I waited for the fourth stroke.

"Return to your class, sir!"

Eucheria was reading to them when I arrived back. I nursed my hand down between the desks and held up my head stoically. In the second last seat of row three, I sat and wondered at the superb cadences of Eucheria's voice. Sometimes, I would secretly touch the palm of the flogged hand with the index finger of the other, and the flesh would tingle excruciatingly. What a triumph it was in itself to shudder with that pain, to hear Eucheria, to have been judged and acquitted with three mere strokes of Stanislaus' ravaging cane. What a triumph it was to live on, and count on one's next breath.

But mostly, until dinnertime, I dreamt of revering Stanilaus who had raised me from the dead. If the school were on fire I would burst into it with a man's strength and haul her black and white serge sacredness into the open air. She would open her eyes in safety and see how much I loved her for her fierce physician's tongue.

After the bell sounded and we escaped to the playground by means of the *standing-like-a-statue* ritual, I sought out Hughie Green, who had a cast in his eye. We walked up towards the Church, to the verge of the out of bounds.

"We're going to go and live at the Cape," I said.

"Where's the Cape?" he wanted to know.

So I told him all I remembered of it.

Two nights before the inquest, the Comrade come home to a completely locked house. He shook the windows and peered inside, but the blinds were down. *She's run through on me*, he told himself. She had pulled the blinds on their bedroom and their lounge room and made him unwelcome to all the house. For half an hour he kicked at the door and worked at all the windows in the laneway. The sublime energies which had driven him to Hilda in the first place, which he believed had been smothered, began again to circle mutely in him. But all he could do for them now that she was gone was to batter at the windows of his and Hilda's dead house. When he got her back, heaven and hell, wouldn't he cherish her!

At half past five he started out for Hilda's parents' place, but the highway was cold and companionship gleamed from the doors of the Meatpackers. In the west, behind dim yellow clouds like snowfields, the sun left for other hemispheres where the summer might be. But it was winter there where the Comrade walked. He shivered, turned into the Meatpackers, asked for whisky, got beer, drank two of them, and decided to go back to Deakin Street and break in.

He smashed the glass in their bedroom window. The bed was made and all was tidy. In the mirror he noticed his own frantic image glancing across the room. The hall had the smell of stale gas, a failure smell of poor food and disenchanted marriage. It was something he detested, and it made him furious at the best of times. By the lounge room he had to push himself through it as though it were a wind which could be measured in miles per hour. He was blind as he opened the kitchen door,

141

and a wall of cooking gas struck his face. Stumbling through the room, he flung open the outside door and lunged out suffocating. After some time he could see again. *Just like a bloody woman*, was all he thought, *going away on a bloke and leaving the gas on*. At length he rushed back into the kitchen to turn off the gas tap and a few feet from the stove fell swearing over Hilda's body.

When he had managed to get the gas out and the light on, he saw Joseph dead on the table with a pillow under his head. There was no pain on his face and a mild academic smile on his forehead. Hilda was on the floor with sticking plaster over her mouth. Why? he wondered. They were both equally dead. They had been dead since early morning.

"Dearest Leonard," Hilda had written in an exercise book open on the table. "It seems we weren't meant for each other. I will love you in hell. I am in a terrible position and I will never get over Lennie getting killed. I made up my mind to send Joseph to God while he's still happy because this world is a rotten place. I love you Len and you are not to grieve. Us going gives you the chance to be the Len Mantle you used to be. We both love you better than our lives.

X X X X X X X X

Your adoring wife,
Hilda.

P.S. — Joseph will not have any pain. I gave him sleeping pills and he's asleep on the table already. I took some myself but I don't know if they will work."

I was not told of any of these events until much later.

17

The Coroner's Court lay amidst pubs and warehouses close to some very deep anchorages. From fifty yards north along the street, you could have thrown stones against the funnels of ships loading for any beleaguered place you might care to name. From these ships, Scandinavians, Lascars, Americans, Scots passed without a glance at the one-storeyed drabness of the court, their eyes on the gaiety of the city a mile up the road. Perhaps across the harbour in Woolloomooloo or up the hill in the Rocks, one of them would be found knifed in the morning. That would be time enough for them to meet the Coroner.

The hearing on the deaths of Dolph (Adolphus Bernard Conlon, minor, to the Court) and Lennie (Leonard George Mantle, minor) began on a morning three weeks after the tragedy. This was the first of two inquests with which the Comrade was to be involved. Hilda's and Joseph's bodies had been released the day before from the morgue fifty yards to the east of the Court. Now their hearing was pending.

The witnesses who waited at five to ten for the Court's public door to open thought mainly of the Comrade, how it must be hell enough even for him to put one's flesh and blood beneath the ground, without having the Court's sterile hands rake the corpses over bone by bone. So beneath the plane trees, the milkman who had been first to the bodies, the red-headed sergeant, my mother, perhaps even the Conlons, were veering in quiet tones towards pity for the Comrade. Until at two minutes to, he came up George Street cleaner, thinner, soberer than we had ever seen him. Immediately faces hardened against him, against the basic indecency of a man who could scarcely manage to look better than a derelict when his family saw him with living eyes, yet came to their inquest as urbanely dressed as for a wedding. He wore a wide black tie, and that was indecently sham; he wore his best tweed coat and that was indecently gay. But above all, he had at his side a pin-striped young barrister, and a man who could care to avoid police prosecution when his follies had consumed his family whole, a man who in those circumstances could go to the trouble of seeking a lawyer's names and, engaging one, stroll off a little chastened and quite upright to the Court with him, that man *was* indecent.

We had been standing in a circle, the Conlons and my mother and I, and Mr Conlon turning his head to look at a merchantman hooting its way out towards Middle Harbour, Mrs Conlon had whispered to my mother, "I had to come with him. If I hadn't, he's just as liable to sit down in a gutter somewhere and cry." On the far side of our group, the Comrade excused himself for a second from his barrister, and sidled into Mr Conlon's line of vision. Perhaps he was contrite or seeking pity or an exchange of pity. Perhaps he was about to make another clumsy attempt at lobbying for some sort of sympathetic support from us in the courtroom, since now, with his whole family vanished in a fortnight, to be arrested would be intolerable. When Mr Conlon saw him he shuddered and then chuckled, as if at some seemly afternoon tea banter on the part of the Comrade.

"Talk about swords being turned back into people's hearts," he grunted, and moved his eyes back to us.

Stell and I were permitted by the Coroner to stay in the witnesses' waiting-room, four walls of aquamarine cheerlessness and a varnished fireplace which had forgotten its purpose. The rules governing witnesses were waived so that I could be guarded from the knowledge that I was now the one survivor of the grenade business. It was not until years later that I found out or wanted to find out how the inquest went for the Comrade. And then the first thing that impressed me was into how delicate a position the red-headed sergeant's family-man sensibilities had betrayed him.

He had not seen fit to bully Hilda and Joseph, he had been prompted to let things ripen for the inquest. Perhaps he had intended to call on them a few days before the inquest and really put the screws on them. In any case, it would have been easy to make Joseph crack amidst the solemnities of an inquest. But now the sergeant's humanity took on an aspect of negligence. Above all, as he sat in the witness box vaguely disturbed by the crown sergeant who acted as prosecutor but was quite brotherly towards him a colleague, as uneasiness tingled beneath his armpits at the Coroner's beginning-of-the-day interest, he must have himself wondered at his own unprofessional kindliness. Without perjuring himself, he had for the sake of his record to ease the Court's attention away from the idea of the Comrade's guilt. For Hilda and Joseph were the only ultimate witnesses to the Comrade's criminality, my evidence being based on hearsay.

After wondering for years why the police had not

sought information from the orange crêpe lady, I found in the Coroner's reports the statement made by the police prosecutor, that incredibly she had died of virus pneumonia two weeks before. Death had had a spree in keeping the Comrade from harm.

After the police sergeant came the reading of the statements of Hilda and Joseph, shaky when given a few weeks before, but astoundingly strong on paper. Joseph had been in terrible shock when the statement was made, and Hilda had refused to leave the room. He had recited the story in which Hilda had schooled him, and the sergeant had had it taken down. Once more, why persecute a terrified eight-year-old semi-cripple? There would be time to let the truth sprout in him.

However, it appears that Joseph did oppose the sergeant's questions with astounding strength of will. He admitted to having told me lies about the origins of the grenade. In fact, he claimed, Lennie and he had found it in the swamps a few weeks before the tragedy. In the company of the sergeant and Hilda, he had pointed at the approximate area where he and his brother had come across it.

"Consider this carefully, sergeant!" the Coroner advised having recalled the sergeant to the stand. "Did the boy seem to you to be telling the truth? Did you believe him?"

"Yes!"

Hilda's statement was that she had never seen the grenade nor heard a hint of it.

Mr Conlon told the court of the Comrade's threat to blow up the Conlon family, but the Comrade's lawyer made Mr Conlon admit that the threat could have easily been a figure of speech, and did not in any definite way point to his client's illegally possessing a grenade.

My mother told the same story and was forced to the

same admission. Any other evidence she attempted to give was branded as hearsay, which must have confused and angered her.

Now there was a ten-minute adjournment which grew to be a twenty-five minute one. It was nearly twelve when the Hamitic-looking constable who was clerk-of-the-court came up to Stell and me as we waited on the steps. He winked at Stell and took me by he shoulder.

"Your turn now, cobber," he grinned with his wide robber baron's mouth. "Don't be frightened. They're all your friends in there, and the Coroner thinks you're a great little bloke."

The Coroner did not look it. Above his grey suit, the face was craggy and wise; his mouth had the petulant upward curve of a mouth which is receiving a sour echo of breakfast. He sat side-on at the crest of a maze of cedar compartments which fanned out from the prosecutor and the shorthand typist to embrace eventually the Press, the witnesses, even the public. In the centre of the court was a large table inhabited by the Comrade's barrister.

The constable led me up to this grim old man on varnished battlements, burping behind his fist as if previous victims sat badly on his stomach. Yet his voice was amazingly soft. It questioned and taught me about oaths, and in the end directed the constable to administer to me an oath that the evidence I would give on behalf of our sovereign Lord the King would be, etc.

The police prosecutor rose as I sat and asked me if I admitted to my name, my address, and the fact that I was a schoolchild. I stared at him and at the shorthand typist, a middle-aged balding male glaring back at me, waiting to tap out my answer. The Coroner laughed dryly.

147

"I think we can take it sergeant, that the witness's answer is *yes*."

One of the two men in the Pressbox lifted his bemused head and grinned painfully for a second.

The prosecutor read my statement as polished by the police stenographer. When he finished there was an unbelieving silence. At last he asked me, "If what you told the police sergeant is the truth, if you believed Mr Mantle had brought home a grenade and was menacing — threatening, you know — his family with it, why didn't you tell anyone?"

"The Comrade would have . . ."

The typist frowned at me in panic. Over the top of the ramparts the Coroner's face appeared.

"Excuse me, Daniel," he said. "But who is this Comrade you mention?"

"Him," I nodded. "Mr Mantle."

"All right. Go on!"

"He would have known it was me who told."

"How would he have known that?" the Coroner asked before the prosecutor could.

Now, glimpsing the Comrade sagging in the corner of the witness's section, all his awesomeness neutralised, I found the Coroner's question hard to answer.

"He thought I was a blabbermouth," I said. A savage joy pushed me forward on the chair. Up here, under the aegis of the Coroner and with my every word being cut into the Court's records, I could harm the Comrade. "When the trucks were stolen, he said he'd kill me if I told anyone."

"What trucks were those?" the prosecutor asked.

"He took Joseph and Lennie . . ."

"That's Joseph Mantle and Lennie Mantle, his sons?" asked the prosecutor lumberingly.

"Yes. He took Joseph and Lennie and me to the corner near the Glasgow Arms, and we saw three trucks of guns and . . . you know, bullets . . . pull up outside the hotel and the drivers went inside. Then six different men came out and stole the trucks."

"Your Worship!" The Comrade's barrister rose. "I can't help but feel that this affects my client's interests, and I must ask for an adjournment to discuss it with him."

"Yes!" said the Coroner and adjourned the Court until two o'clock.

"All rise!" commanded the Hamitic constable.

The after-lunch courtroom was emptier, for the Conlons and the milkman had been permitted to leave. To begin the afternoon, the police prosecutor put a question to me on the Comrade's threat at the time of the truck incident; and then the Coroner asked me if it was because of threats made at that time that I had kept silence over the grenade. At the table, the Comrade's young barrister wrung his hands on the verge of interrupting His Worship.

Now the prosecutor asked me when I had first seen the grenade. Though with a sense of outrage I found it impossible to remember Lennie's face and could evoke only the vaguest flavour even of Joseph's, I found that I knew perfectly the colours, odours, words of that morning when I had first seen the deadly thing in its shoebox. Joseph had seen the Comrade pack it into the cabinet, I said. Here the barrister was allowed to rise and protest that this part of my evidence was hearsay. The Coroner accepted the claim with a deep nod.

"You see," he told me, "we cannot believe everything that people have only heard about. Not everyone is as truthful as you are, you know. All we can take down is what people actually heard or saw themselves. You see, Joseph Mantle might have been lying to you. I mean to say, he did sometimes tell lies didn't he, as most boys actually do?''

''Sometimes,'' I piped, though I couldn't remember when.

All day the Coroner had presented his bored, clinical gaze to the question of Dolph's and Lennie's death by blast. The voice had been fluent, concerned, alive, but the face dead. Yet now he continued to survey me for a long ten seconds, mild alarm crinkling the corners of his eyes. He was genuinely disturbed that a child should think the Coroner's Court to be armoured against the truth.

''When was the next time you saw the grenade?'' the police prosecutor asked.

The first night; Joseph drenched at the window; plucking the detonator out. They wanted to know of course, how I'd learnt about the detonator, and I explained how Matt had been pumped.

It was the Comrade's barrister's turn, and he rose and took up once more the plaint of hearsay. There was no evidence, he said, for the truth of the tale which Joseph had given me, of the Comrade's sitting the family around his Mills bomb while he entered on a dialogue with it. Hilda Mantle's statement denied it.

However long in the forgetting, the rest of the affair was quickly, anti-climactically told. In the end, the Coroner thanked me, assured me that the truth would be found, regretted that I might have to be called back to the stand, and permitted me to wait out the rest of the hearing in the witnesses' waiting-room.

Stell and I spent the remainder of the inquest there. The sun must have slipped behind the warehouses across the street, and the little chamber was dim and as cold as a gully. Grey light, the colour of boredom, oozed through the opened tops of windows glazed with a large crown and the words *City Coroner* in gothic.

But we were in holiday mood. For us it sufficed that the inquest was all but finished, that by the weekend we would be at the Cape. I asked every now and then, with a kind of gaseous unease in my chest, if Joseph blamed me, and Stell persisted that of course he didn't. I would have to see him, I said, before I went.

"We'll have to see," Stell murmured. "He hasn't been well. He might be away. But he doesn't blame you. You were all trying to save people. It was the Comrade who killed Lennie and Dolph. Because the Comrade bought that grenade especially to kill. It was the Comrade who committed murder in his heart. You and Joseph and Lennie were foolish. The thing is, not to mean harm."

She talked on about the Cape; sharks in knee-deep water mad with hunger on Fourteen Mile Beach, a whale up on the sand and too big to cart away, the ghosts . . . since it is better to be frightened than bored . . . of dead convicts on Warialda. And at last, about five the courtroom door opened and the boots of the interested parties clumped in the corridor. I rushed to the door to see the Comrade and his lawyer hurry out. Then the red-haired sergeant came strolling along deflatedly.

"What's the verdict?" Stell asked him.

"Death by misadventure!" he said.

"What about the Comrade?"

He shrugged and screwed up his cheeks. "There's no evidence against him. They might question him. But in the end there's no evidence."

"Anyhow," he continued, safe, fat, glibly pious, peering out into the dusk, "he's been punished by a *greater One* than the Coroner."

A glazed window glimmered as a light went by under the trees.

"It's going to be confounded cold tonight," he remarked.